"Oh, I'm so sorry!" Brianna automatically apologized, stepping back and trying to collect herself.

She felt slightly flustered, but did her best not to show it.

"No, it was totally my fault," Sebastian said, annoyed with himself. Drawing back, he'd automatically reached out to steady the woman he'd nearly sent sprawling. He caught her by her slender shoulders. The next moment, his vision clearing, enabling him to actually focus on the face of the woman before him, he dropped his hands from her shoulders, stunned.

At the same time, Sebastian's jaw dropped.

The one person he hadn't wanted to run into at the reunion was standing less than five inches away from him.

Looking far more radiant than he ever remembered her looking.

Dear Reader,

Matchmaking Mamas was supposed to be a three-book series with three lifelong friends joining forces to get their three daughters married. Since I am never one to let something go (just ask my husband), I decided to keep the series going for another book or two—or six.

This time, what came to mind was my own beloved editor's fairy-tale romance. The young man she danced with at a prom contacted her twenty-six years later just to see how she was doing. Life had taken them on separate paths, literally halfway around the world from one another. "Catching up" led to lengthy phone calls, to a visit, to a relocation and then, best of all, to "happily ever after." How could I *not* write about that?

Patience and Sam became my inspiration for this book. I am forever grateful that they shared this story with me and, most important of all, that they came back into one another's lives and proved that second chances *are* possible and that optimism is *not* baseless. Happy Forever, Patience and Sam.

As always, I thank you for reading, and from the bottom of my heart I wish you someone to love who loves you back.

All the best,

Marie Ferrarella

TEN YEARS LATER...

MARIE FERRARELLA

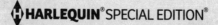

HARLEQUIN® SPECIAL EDITION®

Recycling programs
for this product may
not exist in your area.

ISBN-13: 978-0-373-65734-6

TEN YEARS LATER...

Printed in U.S.A.

MARIE FERRARELLA

This *USA TODAY* bestselling and RITA® Award-winning author has written more than two hundred books for Harlequin Books, some under the name Marie Nicole. Her romances are beloved by fans worldwide. Visit her website, www.marieferrarella.com.

To
Patience Bloom
and
her Sam,
who were my inspiration
for this story.
Thank you.

Prologue

"Maizie, may I speak with you?"

Maizie Sommer looked up from her desk and watched the approach of the sweet-faced, heavyset woman who'd just entered her real estate office.

She knew that look. She'd seen it before, more than once. Not in her capacity as a remarkably successful Realtor with her own agency, but in her role as an even *more* successful matchmaker.

What had begun several years ago as a determined plan to get her own daughter—and the daughters of her two best friends—matched up and married to their soul mates had turned into a calling.

Since the first time she had gone down this path, Maizie, along with Theresa Manetti and Cecilia Parnell, all three best friends since the third grade, had never encountered failure. Strong gut instincts had guided the three women as they played matchmakers for friends and relatives, unerringly pairing up their targets, not for profit but for the sheer love of it.

As they amassed one triumphant pairing after another, their reputations grew. So much so that at times, their businesses were forced to take a temporary backseat to what Maizie liked to refer to as their "true mission."

"Come in, Barbara," Maizie said warmly. Rising, she turned the chair in front of her desk so that the visitor could easily take a seat. "So tell me, what can I do for you?"

Barbara Hunter, whose fondness for rich, good food was evident, sank down into the proffered chair. The retired high school English teacher sighed wearily. This was something she'd been wrestling with for a long time. Coming to Maizie for help amounted to a last-ditch effort before she completely gave up.

"You can tell me how to light a fire under my stubborn son."

Maizie looked at the other woman, puzzled. "I'm afraid I don't—"

Anticipating her friend's question, Barbara elaborated. "He was supposed to come home for his high school's ten-year reunion, but now he tells me that he doesn't have time for that 'nonsense,'—his word, not mine—and that he wants to save that time and put it toward his Christmas vacation so that when he *does* come out, we can have a nice, long visit."

Soft brown eyes shifted imploringly toward Maizie. "Oh, Maizie, I had such hopes for him…." Barbara's voice trailed off, lost in another deep sigh.

Maizie, meanwhile, was busy cataloging information. "Remind me, where's your son now?"

"Sebastian is in Japan, teaching Japanese businessmen how to speak English. He's really very good at it," she interjected with visible pride. "When he skipped his five-year reunion, he told me that he'd attend the next milestone reunion 'for sure.' His words," she said again, more bleakly this time. She looked like a woman clinging to the last vestiges of hope and trying to make peace with the knowledge that it was slipping through her fingers. "I was hoping he'd go to this one and maybe even get together with Brianna."

The name seemed to just wistfully hang there. "Brianna?" Maizie prodded.

Barbara nodded. "Brianna MacKenzie, the girl Sebastian went with during his senior year. I have this beautiful prom picture of the two of them," she confided, then added with feeling, "A lovely, lovely girl. I really thought that they'd wind up getting married, but Sebastian went off to college and Brianna stayed behind to take care of her father. The poor man was involved in a terrible car accident the night of the prom. She literally nursed him back to health and was so good at it, she went on to become an actual nurse."

Barbara closed her eyes and shook her head as she felt the last nail being hammered into the coffin of her dreams.

"I had hoped..." Her voice trailed off, but it wasn't hard to fill in the blanks. "Now Sebastian's apparently changed his mind again. I'm beginning to think that I'm never going to see my son get married, much less hold a grandchild in my arms. Sebastian's my only boy, Maizie. My only child. I've tried to be patient. Lord knows I haven't interfered in his life, but I don't have forever. Do you have *any* suggestions?" she asked, clearly counting on a miracle.

The wheels in Maizie's head were already turning and she was lost in thought. "How's that again?" she asked, focusing intently.

"Do you have any suggestions?" Barbara Hunter repeated.

But Maizie shook her head. "No, not that. What did you say just before that?" she coaxed.

Barbara paused and thought. "That I don't want to interfere in his life?" She had no idea what Maizie was after.

Maizie frowned, shaking her head. "No, *after* that," she stressed.

Barbara paused again, thinking for a moment longer. "That I don't have forever?" It was purely a guess at this point.

Maizie smiled broadly. "That's it."

Barbara looked at her uncertainly, completely lost. "*What's* it?"

The pieces were all coming together. Maizie almost beamed. "That's how you're going to get Sebastian to come home—and incidentally, to attend the reunion."

Barbara struggled to follow what her friend was saying, but it wasn't easy. "I think that Sebastian already suspects I'm not immortal."

"To suspect is one thing—we all know no one lives forever—but to suddenly come up against that jarring fact is quite another." She watched Barbara expectantly, throwing the ball back into her court.

Barbara came to the only conclusion she could. "You want me to tell Sebastian I'm dying?" Even as she said it, it sounded surreal.

"Not dying, Barbara," Maizie corrected gently. "You're going to tell your son that you had 'an episode.'"

It still didn't make any sense. "An episode? An episode of what?"

"Well, definitely not an episode of *NCIS: Los Angeles,*" Maizie told her with a patient smile. "If I remember correctly, Bedford High is celebrating a graduating class's tenth reunion in ten days, right?"

That her friend had this sort of information at her fingertips caught Barbara off guard. She knew that Maizie's daughter hadn't gone to that school and knew of no reason why the woman should be aware that the high school was throwing another reunion party.

"How do you know?"

"How do I know that?" Maizie guessed. She loved being on top of things. "It just so happens that Theresa Manetti was talking about landing the catering assignment for that party just the other day. But never mind that for now. You just call that son of yours and tell him that you don't want to alarm him but that you might have had a minor stroke, and that you'd really rather not put off seeing him, 'just in case.'"

"But I'll be lying to Sebastian and that's a bad lie," Barbara protested uncomfortably.

Maizie looked at her innocently. "Then you *do* want to put off seeing him?"

"No, of course not. That part's true enough, but I haven't had a stroke, light or otherwise," Barbara underscored.

Maizie quoted a statistic. "Did you know that, according to a report I recently read, some people actually have strokes and never realize it?"

"No, I didn't kn—" Barbara held the information highly suspect. "Maizie, are you stretching the truth?"

"No, not stretching, Barbara, but you of all people must know that communication is all about how you use your words. It's not what you say but how you say it," she told the other woman with a broad smile. "You have to be ruthless if you want your son to come home."

Barbara still seemed uncomfortable about the untruth. "I don't know, Maizie…."

"You don't know if you want to see your son happily married and starting a family?" Maizie asked.

"No, of course I do," Barbara said with feeling. And got no further.

Maizie could feel her adrenaline beginning to surge. She *loved* a challenge—and this had the makings of a really good one.

"Good. Then let me look into a few things and I'll get right back to you. With the reunion so close, we don't have that much time. In the meanwhile, you get that son of yours on the phone and tell him that you *really* want to see him now. That you'd rather not wait until Christmas—just in case. Understood?"

Barbara nodded. "Understood." She only hoped that, in the long run, Sebastian would find it in his heart to forgive her.

Chapter One

Sebastian Hunter felt exhausted as he and the three hundred and twelve other passengers packed closely around him ended their eleven-and-a-half-hour international flight by finally getting off the plane at LAX.

Concerned ever since he'd gotten off the phone with his mother a scant two days ago, he'd been far too wired even to catnap on the flight, which had covered more than five thousand miles and had taken him from the heart of Tokyo to Los Angeles.

It didn't help matters any that there was a sixteen-hour time difference between the two cities, not to mention that he felt as if he'd been traveling backward. He'd left Tokyo early on Saturday morning only to arrive in Los Angeles late Friday night, which technically made it the night before.

And he wasn't done yet.

There was still customs to go through, despite the fact that he had brought nothing with him to declare. He'd packed hastily, informed his employer of the family emergency that necessitated his presence and arranged for a leave of absence. And now, perilously close to fraying his very last nerve—because airport security had the passengers as well as its staff on edge—he was forced to pretend he was cool, calm and collected. Otherwise, if he allowed any of the tension he was feeling to show, he might just find himself detained far longer than it would take to queue up for a random search. Tense passengers were regarded with suspicion.

He struggled to curb his impatience, although he was losing the battle.

C'mon, c'mon, how long are you going to spend going through her underwear? he wondered irritably as the customs agent rifled through a young woman's suitcase.

The process seemed to take forever. Where were Dorothy's ruby-red slippers when you needed them, Sebastian thought darkly.

The phrase echoed in his brain, startling him. God, he had to *really* be punchy if he was thinking about donning the fairy-tale footwear just to get him home.

His mind was going—and that was in part thanks to his lack of sleep.

But he wasn't in a hurry because of fatigue. He was in a hurry because, for the first time in his life, at the age of twenty-nine, he had become acutely aware of mortality.

Not his own. The thought of not being around someday didn't bother him in the slightest. What would be would be, as his mother always liked to say.

However, somewhere in the back of his mind, he'd grown comfortable with the concept of always having his mother around. His image of her had stabilized somewhere between what she'd looked like when he'd last seen her and a little older than an actress she had always admired, Barbara Stanwyck, playing the matriarch of a large family. To him his mother was—and always had been—proud, determined and incredibly capable.

He knew the image wasn't eternal and certainly not realistic, but he couldn't entertain the idea that his mother would someday decline and eventually cease to be. Nor did he want to.

He would have traded in his soul to be able to break into a run, make time stand still and miraculously appear at her side the moment he hung up the phone, ending the unexpected, unnerving call he'd received from her.

And now it seemed as if it had been forever before Sebastian was finally standing outside the terminal where he had deplaned, signaling to the closest taxi driver that he needed a ride to get to his final destination.

He hoped, because the hour was so late, that for once he would be spared having to deal with an infamous

Los Angeles traffic jam. But it was also Friday night, which meant that everyone was out on the road.

Being as sprawled out as Los Angeles was, nothing was ever close by and thus necessitated obligatory travel from one point to the next, which in turn, like as not, resulted in gridlock.

"Business or pleasure?" the gypsy cabdriver asked him as they found themselves inching along the San Diego Freeway.

Preoccupied, trying not to worry about his mother, Sebastian barely heard the question. Looking up, his eyes met the driver's in the rearview mirror. "What?"

"Are you here on business or pleasure?" the man repeated, looking to kill some time by striking up a conversation.

"Neither."

How did you categorize flying halfway around the world to ascertain whether or not your only living relative, the mother you loved, would be around to welcome in another year? It still felt very surreal to him.

"Oh," the driver muttered in response, obviously taking the answer to mean that his passenger didn't want to be communicative.

Sebastian thought of saying something inane to show the driver that he wasn't trying to be rude, but decided if he did that, it might leave him open to an onslaught of conversation. He allowed the silence within the vehicle to continue by default.

Outside the gypsy cab, the typical sounds of engines, horns and vehicles whose drivers were impatient to reach their destinations echoed through the night air like a bad symphony.

Sebastian tried to relax.

He couldn't.

Despite the fact that the house in Bedford where he had grown up was located only forty-five miles from the airport, it took him over two hours to reach it. But eventually, Sebastian could finally make out the silhouette of the familiar two-story building.

In his hurry to get out, Sebastian gave the driver a fistful of bills he'd pulled out of his wallet. The man's pleased grunt in response told him that he had probably well exceeded the amount due, even when taking a generous tip into account.

Pocketing the money, the cabdriver jumped out of the vehicle, quickly removed the carry-on luggage and set it on the sidewalk. In two seconds, he was back behind the wheel and driving swiftly away, as if he was afraid that his fare would suddenly change his mind and take back some of the cash.

Alone, Sebastian stood and looked at the dark house where he'd lived for all his formative years.

The relentless sense of urgency that had dogged his every move throughout the five and a half thousand miles slipped into the background, pushed there by a very real, gnawing fear that once he was in his mother's company, he would hear something he wasn't prepared to hear.

He knew he wasn't being realistic, but as long as the details were not out in the open, he could pretend that they didn't exist, or at the very least, that they were better than he'd been led to believe.

Sebastian frowned in the dark.

Since when had he become such a coward? he silently demanded. He'd always gone full-steam ahead, hiding from nothing, consequences be damned. His philosophy had *always* been that it was far better to know than not to know. That way, he felt that he was always prepared for anything.

Yes, but this is your mother, your home port. Your rock. The cornerstone of who and what you are.

He was, he realized, afraid of losing her. His mother had always been the one steadfast thing in his life. She was why he felt free to roam, to explore the depths and extent of the possibilities of his life. As long as she was there to anchor him, to return to, he felt free to fly as high as he wanted.

But if she wasn't there...

Grow up, Hunter, Sebastian ordered himself.

He left it at that, not wanting to follow his thought to its logical conclusion. Instead, he made up his mind that if his mother needed him, he would be there for her, no matter what it took, just as she had always been there for him.

From the time that he was five years old, it had been just the two of them. It was time that he paid her back for that. For all the support, emotional and otherwise, that she had so willingly, so freely given him.

Exhaling a long breath, he braced himself. Sebastian

slipped his hand into his right pocket, feeling around for a moment.

His fingers curled around a very familiar object.

His house key.

He always kept the key on his person—for luck more than anything else. But now he held it in his hand, intending to use it for its true purpose: to get him inside his house.

For a moment, he considered doing just that. Unlocking the door, walking in and surprising his mother. But given the fact that she had suffered a recent, mild— God, he hoped it was truly just that—stroke, surprising her like that might bring on a heart attack—or worse. Most likely not, but he was not about to take a chance on even a remote possibility of that happening.

So he took out his cell phone and pressed the second preprogrammed number on his keypad. A moment later, he heard the phone on the other end ringing.

Two more rings and then a sleepy voice mumbled, "Hello?"

Why was he choking up just at the sound of her voice? He wasn't going to be a help to anyone if he kept tearing up, he admonished himself.

"Hi, Mom."

"Sebastian!" Besides instant recognition, there was also an instant smile evident in her voice. "Where are you?"

"I'm right outside your front door, Mom," he answered.

"My front door?" she echoed, suddenly wide awake. "Here?"

"You have another front door I should know about?" Sebastian joked.

She sounded great. Just the way she always did. Maybe there'd been some mix-up, he thought hopefully. Maybe she hadn't had a stroke. After all, her blood work had always been good.

So good, in fact, that it had been the source of envy among her friends.

His mother had always been the healthiest woman he'd ever known. Which made this news so much harder for him to accept.

Barbara didn't answer her son's question. Instead, she said, "Well, don't just stand there, Sebastian. Come in, come in," she urged.

Before Sebastian could pick up his suitcase and cross from the curb to the tall, stained-glass front door, it all but flew open. His mother, wearing the ice-blue robe he'd sent her last Christmas, her salt-and-pepper hair a slightly messy, fluffy halo around her head, was standing in the doorway, her arms outstretched, waiting for her only son to fill them.

Sebastian stepped forward, ready to embrace his mother. But when he reached out to her, he almost wound up stepping on a very indignant gray-and-white-striped cat that was weaving itself in and out between his legs.

The cat was not shy about voicing her displeasure at having to put up with an intruder in her well-organized little world.

Sebastian pretended to take no notice of the feline as he bent over and hugged his mother. Relief surged through him like unleashed adrenaline.

"Come in, come in," Barbara urged eagerly, stepping back into her living room.

As Sebastian took a step forward, the cat again wove in and out between his legs, narrowly avoiding getting into a collision with him.

When he almost tripped on the furry animal, he frowned more deeply. He looked down at the offending territorial creature with sharp claws.

"When did you get a cat?" he asked. His mother had never been one for pets, and he had grown up without one.

"Don't you recognize her, Sebastian?" Barbara asked in surprise.

He shrugged. "Sorry. You've seen one cat, you've seen them all," he tossed out casually.

"He doesn't mean that, Marilyn," she told the cat in a soothing voice. Turning toward her son, she said, "That's the kitten you gave me before you left for Japan. She's grown some," she added needlessly.

"Grown 'some'?" he questioned incredulously, looking back at the cat. The cat looked as if she could benefit from a week's stay at a health spa. "She's as big as a house."

"Don't hurt her feelings, Sebastian," his mother requested. "She can understand everything that we say about her."

A highly skeptical expression passed over his face.

As much as he would have liked to humor his mother, there had to be a line drawn somewhere. He fixed the cat with a look meant to hold her in place for a moment.

"Get out of the way, cat." The feline didn't budge. Sebastian grinned as he turned to his mother. "Apparently not everything."

"Oh, she understands," Barbara maintained good-naturedly. "She just chooses not to listen, that's all. Not unlike a little boy I used to know," his mother concluded with affection.

Sebastian brought in his suitcase, leaving it next to the doorway. He closed the door, then paused and took full measure of his mother, after she'd turned on the lights inside the room.

"Mom," Sebastian began, partly confused, partly relieved, "you look good. You look *very* good," he underscored. "How do you feel?"

It was then that Barbara remembered she was supposed to be playing a part. For a minute, seeing her son standing there on her doorstep, every other thought had fled from her mind. As she considered what she was about to say, the deception threatened to gag her. But then she recalled the afternoon of coaching she'd undergone with Maizie. The matchmaker had seemed so sure of the outcome of all this.

She *had* to give it a chance.

"I don't feel as good as I look, I'm afraid. Makeup does wonders."

Now that was a new one. "Since when do you wear makeup to bed?"

"Since I had to call nine-one-one in the middle of the night," she answered primly.

"You do realize that when they respond, they're here to possibly take you to the hospital, not escort you to a party," he told her.

"I didn't want them to have to see an ugly old lady," she said simply.

"You're not an ugly old lady, Mom. You're a pretty old lady," he said, tongue in cheek.

"Remind me to hit you when I get better," she answered.

That had been the test. Had she taken a swipe at him, the way she had in the past when the teasing between them had escalated, he would have felt that perhaps there'd been a false alarm, that she was really all right.

But her restraint told him the exact opposite. That she *wasn't* all right.

He pressed a kiss to her temple. "You're not an old lady, Mom. You know that. You look younger than women fifteen years younger than you are."

She smiled at him, grateful for the compliment, even though she knew it was a huge exaggeration.

"Nevertheless, a lady should always look her best," she maintained.

He shook his head, but unlike the old days, this time it was affection rather than impatience that filled him. That was his mother, determined to look her best no matter what the situation. He had to admire that kind of strong will.

And then he realized what she'd just told him. "You had to call nine-one-one?"

This was just going to be the first of many lies, Barbara thought, even as she reminded herself that it was all for an ultimate greater good.

"Yes. But it wasn't so bad, dear," she assured him. "The young men took very good care of me."

There was genuine regret in his eyes. "I'm sorry I wasn't here for you, Mom."

She patted his hand, the simple gesture meant to absolve him of any blame. "Don't give it another thought. You have your own life, Sebastian. And besides, you're here now and that's what counts," she added.

"So tell me everything," he urged. "What did the doctor say?"

"We can talk about all that tomorrow," she told him, waving away his request. "Tonight I just want to look at you. You still like coffee?" she asked suddenly, then turning on her heel, she began to lead the way to the kitchen. "Or have you decided to switch to green tea now?"

"I still like coffee," he answered.

"Nice to know that some things don't change," she told him.

Yes, but most things do, he thought, following behind her.

As the thought sank in, he could feel his heart aching. He should have come home a lot more, he upbraided himself. Even if coming home reminded him of all the things he'd given up and all the things he still didn't have, he should have come home more often.

"Sure you're up to this?" he asked his mother, concerned.

Barbara turned on the overhead lights, throwing the small, light blue kitchen into daylight.

"Putting water into a coffee urn? I think so," she deadpanned. "And if for some reason I can't, as I recall, you can."

And then she paused to hook both her arms through his for a moment and just squeeze him to her.

"Oh, it's so good to have you here. You're just the best medicine I could ask for."

Her words both gladdened his heart and pierced it with guilt. He switched the topic.

"Marilyn, huh?" The animal in question had followed them to the kitchen and had now positioned herself directly by the refrigerator, like a furry sentry who wanted to be paid in fish scraps. "Why Marilyn?"

"After Marilyn Monroe," Barbara answered without any hesitation. "Because when she crosses a room, she moves her hips just like Marilyn Monroe did in *Some Like It Hot*."

Sebastian pressed his lips together, knowing that his mother wouldn't appreciate his laughing at her explanation. All he trusted himself to say, almost under his breath, was "If you say so, Mom."

Turning away to look at the cat, he missed seeing the look of satisfaction that fleetingly passed over his mother's face.

Chapter Two

"You look pretty, Mama."

Brianna turned from the full-length mirror in her bedroom and glanced at the slightly prejudiced short person who had just uttered those flattering words. Sweet though it was, it wasn't the compliment that had warmed her heart; it was what the little girl had called her.

Mama.

She wondered if she would ever get used to hearing that particular word addressed to her.

Certainly she knew that she'd never take it for granted, especially since, biologically speaking, she wasn't Carrie's mother.

But there was no denying that presently she was the four-year-old's only family. She and her father, who, mercifully, had taken to the role of grandfather like the proverbial duck to water. He liked nothing better than doting on the curly-haired small girl and, in effect, being her partner in crime. Not only was Carrie precocious and the personification of energy, she also possessed a *very* active imagination.

"Least I can do after all you've done for me, Bree," he'd told her when she'd commented on the unusual dynamics their family had taken on.

"You are my dad," she reminded him, dismissing the need for any gratitude or words of thanks. "What was I supposed to do, just walk away and leave you to fend for yourself?"

He'd smiled at her. Brianna had never been one to take credit for anything. "A lot of other kids would have," he'd pointed out. "And not many would have postponed their education—and their life," he emphasized, recalling everything that had been involved that terrible summer when she'd stayed behind to nurse him after his horrific car accident.

An accident that his doctors insisted would leave him totally paralyzed, if not a comatose vegetable. Brianna had been his one-woman cheering section, refusing to allow him to wallow in self-pity or give in to the almost crippling pain. Instead, she'd worked him like a heartless straw boss. He gave up every day, but not Brianna.

She'd kept insisting that he was going to walk away from his wheelchair no matter what his doctors said to the contrary. She took nursing courses and physical therapy courses, all with a single focus in mind: to get him to walk again.

And during whatever downtime she had, between working with him and studying, she'd pitched in to help run his hardware store, working with his partner, J.T., whenever the latter needed to have some slack picked up.

By Jim MacKenzie's accounting, his daughter hadn't slept for more than a couple of hours a night for close to three years. The day he'd taken those first shaky steps away from his wheelchair, he remembered that she'd looked at him with tears in her eyes, a radiant smile on her lips, and declared, "Looks like I can go to bed now."

Brianna now looked at the little girl who was sitting on her bed, waving her feet back and forth as if channeling out her energy to the world at large.

"Thank you, baby," Brianna said to the child she'd come to love as her own.

"She doesn't look pretty, Carrie," Jim informed the little girl as he left his post in the doorway and walked into the room to join the two women in his life. "She looks *beautiful*."

Brianna's eyes met her father's. A knowing smile curved her lips. "I'm onto you, you know. You're just saying that because you want me to go to this silly reunion."

In his own way, her father was as stubborn as she was. He didn't believe in giving an inch. "I'm just saying it because it's true—and because I want you to go out and have a good time."

He was up to something and she knew it. "Then let's go to the movies," she suggested. "The three of us. My treat," she added to sweeten the pot.

"Number one—" he ticked off on his fingers "—the movies aren't going anywhere—they'll always be there. Number two, even if I said yes to going, I don't need you paying for my ticket. I'm the dad. I get to take the two of you out."

Brianna seized the moment. "Great—let's go."

His eyes told her he wasn't about to budge from his position. "But not tonight," he continued, remaining firm. "Go, catch up with your friends," he coaxed, then predicted, "It'll be fun."

Brianna sighed and shook her head, her light auburn hair swirling about her face like a pale red cloud. "Spoken like a man who has never had to attend any of his high school reunions."

Carrie puckered her small face, a sure sign that she was trying to absorb the conversation around her. Given a choice, the little girl always preferred the company of adults to that of children her own age. She knew that adults occasionally even forgot that she was there, but she didn't mind. She was content just to sit there, listening to them talk.

She was truly a sponge. Soaking up everything, her curiosity constantly being aroused.

"What's a higher reunion?" she asked, looking from her grandfather to the woman she thought of as her mother.

"High *school* reunion," Brianna corrected. "That's

when a bunch of people who used to go to the same classes together hold a party every few years so that they can pretend to be successful, making people jealous of them while they're checking who got fat and who lost their hair."

Carrie was quiet for a moment, then observed, "Doesn't sound like much fun."

Her point eloquently stated, Brianna looked at her father as she gestured toward Carrie. "Out of the mouths of babes."

Carrie's lower lip stuck out just a shade as she protested, "I'm not a baby."

"Maybe not," Brianna allowed, giving the girl a quick hug, "but you're *my* baby."

"And you're mine," Jim informed her firmly, but with the same underlying note of love. "Now, shake a leg and get to this thing before it's over."

Brianna grinned, pretending to weigh the thought. "Now, *there's* an idea. If I take my time getting ready and move really slowly, this lame reunion will be over by the time I get there."

"I hereby declare you ready," Jim announced, taking her by the hand and drawing her to the stairs. Carrie was quick to grab her other hand and follow suit, her blue eyes dancing. "I'm all set to babysit and you look fantastic. You have no excuse," Jim concluded, his words firmly declaring that the discussion—or argument—was officially over.

Giving in, Brianna allowed herself to be led down the stairs. Once on the ground floor, she raised her hands in semisurrender. She gave her father her compromise.

"I'll go—but I'll be home early," she told him.

He wasn't through bargaining. "You'll be home late and like it," he countered. Putting his wide, hamlike hands to her back, he aimed her at the front door and gave her a little push. "Now *go*."

This time, it was an order.

With a sigh, Brianna gave in. In the long run, it was easier that way. Kissing Carrie and then her father goodbye, she left.

Her CR-V, the car that J.T. had left to her upon his incredibly untimely death, was parked in the driveway and she crossed to it.

According to the very short will, J.T. had stated that the vehicle was an inadequate thank-you present. Though it wasn't spelled out, Brianna knew he was thanking her for saying that she would be Carrie's guardian in the event that something happened to him.

And then "something" had.

A week before their quickly planned wedding, J.T. had died in what amounted to a freak boating accident.

All throughout the funeral, she couldn't help thinking of the old adage J.T. had always been fond of quoting: If you wanted to make God laugh, tell Him you've started making plans.

She certainly hadn't planned for it to be this way. She had a daughter—and a CR-V—and no husband, no shot at attaining "happily ever after."

It was the second time that had happened to her.

Was that it? she wondered suddenly. Was that why she kept attending these damn reunions?

Was that why she'd let her father talk her into attending this one?

Because deep down inside, was she hoping that the first man who had made her yearn for a "happily ever after" before it had all turned to dust might attend this reunion?

As she drove down the brightly lit streets, she reminded herself that Sebastian Hunter hadn't attended the last reunion. Why in heaven's name did she think he was going to attend this one?

And even if he did, a little voice in her head mocked her, *are you going to rush up to him, throw your arms around him and say, "Let's pick up where we left off"?*

"No, of course not," Brianna said tersely, defensively, giving voice to her thoughts out loud.

Brianna took in a deep breath and unconsciously squared her shoulders as she came to a stop at a red light. Annoyed at the path her thoughts were taking, she reminded herself that she was made of sterner stuff than that. She hadn't cracked up when her father had almost died in that car accident—she'd stuck by him and done what had to be done.

And she hadn't cracked up when the guy she loved more than anything on earth had left her behind to go to college, emotionally stranding her and growing progressively more and more distant until he'd finally just completely disappeared from her life.

She hadn't even given up and booked a ride on the SS *Catatonic* when J.T. was killed.

Instead, she'd faced each and every one of her challenges, emerging whole on the other side. Moreover, she knew she would continue to face her challenges, determined to come out the victor no matter what dragon she was forced to battle.

Raising her head up a little higher, Brianna drove on.

Sebastian frowned behind his near-empty wineglass. He still couldn't believe that he had actually wound up here, despite his determination not to set foot into this sad little affair.

He was here because his mother had begged him to attend. Face-to-face with those incredibly sad eyes of hers, he found that the word *no* just refused to emerge.

Sebastian was far from happy about this unexpected turn of events.

But it was all his own fault. He couldn't blame anyone else for his being here right now. The blame rested squarely on his own shoulders. He'd been so desperate to do anything to please his infirm mother, he'd made the mistake of saying as much—and this, *this,* was the only thing she asked of him. To attend his high school reunion—and then come home and tell her all about it in the morning.

Except that there wasn't all that much to tell, he thought, slowly looking around and taking in the various little cliques gathered together throughout the large room.

Apparently the "mean kids" were now "mean adults," and the "nice kids" were still their targets, even though they were now, for the most part, "nice adults."

And, he noted, the ones who went on to make something of themselves and become successful had skipped the reunion entirely.

Just as he should have done.

Just as he had intended on doing until he'd been informed of his mother's stroke.

Okay, so he was here now because he'd promised his mother he would attend. However, he hadn't told her how *long* he'd be staying, so the duration of this Chinese water torture was strictly up to him.

Sebastian glanced at his watch. Nine o'clock. As good a time as any to declare that his stint in hell was officially over.

Draining the last bit of punch from the glass he'd been holding on to for the past hour—at least the food and drink had been excellent—Sebastian put the empty glass down on one of the side tables.

Time for a swift exit.

He looked neither to the left nor to the right, afraid that if he accidentally made eye contact with anyone he might be forced to spend an extra few minutes engaged in stilted, polite conversation with a person he would only pretend to remember.

It was exactly because he was avoiding making any sort of possible eye contact that he didn't see her.

Not until they had collided.

At that point, they were just two bodies with definite goals in mind and gaits that resembled slightly disoriented gazelles attempting to flee their unwanted location.

"Oh, I'm so sorry!" Brianna automatically apologized, stepping back and trying to collect herself. She felt slightly flustered, but did her best not to show it.

"No, it was totally my fault," Sebastian said, annoyed with himself for being so preoccupied that he'd been oblivious of where he was going.

Mercifully, at least there were no small, half-filled glasses of red punch to christen the unplanned collision. He really didn't want to remain here one more moment than he already had. So far, he hadn't really run into anyone he knew and for simplicity's sake, and the sake of a clean getaway, he wanted to keep it that way.

Drawing back, he reached out to steady the woman he'd nearly sent sprawling. He caught her by her slender shoulders. The next moment, his vision clearing, enabling him to actually focus on the face of the woman before him, he dropped his hands from her shoulders, stunned.

At the same time, Sebastian's jaw dropped.

The one person he hadn't wanted to run into at the reunion was standing less than five inches away from him.

Looking far more radiant than he ever remembered her looking.

Maybe he was wrong.

Maybe it wasn't her.

"Bree?" He cleared his throat and this time managed to say her full name. It came out in the form of a question. "Brianna?"

And even as he said her name, he tried to convince himself that he was mistaken. That he had just bumped into someone who merely reminded him of the girl he'd left behind.

The girl who had, in effect, emotionally stranded him, leaving him adrift.

Brianna could feel her stomach sinking—and fervently wished that the rest of her could go, too. Straight down through a hole in the ground.

But the floor remained solid even as her stomach twisted into a knot, making it hard for her even to breathe.

Her chin shot up as she squared her shoulders, looking for all the world like a soldier prepared to face certain death.

"Sebastian?"

The way Brianna said his name had always made him smile. Half lecture, half prayer. That much, he thought, hadn't changed.

But everything else *had,* he silently stressed. He'd gone on to make a life for himself abroad. A very good life.

If it, coincidentally, was also a solitary life, well, that had been his choice, right? Had he stayed behind or at least waited for her, instead of beginning to cut ties practically from the start, maybe life would have turned out differently.

But there was no way of really knowing just how

things would have gone, and besides, he had no *real* regrets. He didn't *allow* himself to have any. He'd chosen to leave Bedford and grow, rather than to remain here and stagnate.

"You look good," he heard himself saying to her.

God, talk about inane lines. But his mind had gone blank. Either that, or abruptly missing in action.

But she did look good, he had to admit. Maybe even *too* good. He didn't remember her figure being quite this curvy. And he was in a position to know. The last day they had been together, he'd shared the last dance at the prom with her. It had been a slow number and he'd held her to him for what had felt like an eternity.

Maybe you would have held her for far longer if you had actually remained in Bedford.

He blocked out the voice.

"You, too," Brianna was saying.

Her mouth felt dry, as if it was incapable of sustaining or uttering a single word without her tongue sticking to the roof of her mouth.

She cleared her throat, searching for a graceful way to end this awkward moment. A moment that *shouldn't* have been awkward at all.

Sebastian had been her first love, and her first lover.

Her pulse was racing. That couldn't be good, she thought.

"Were you just leaving?" Brianna finally managed to ask. *When at a loss for words, go with the truth,* she told herself.

"No." The denial was purely automatic. Relenting

just a little, he murmured, "Maybe." But that was obviously a lie. So he finally admitted, "Yes."

The fluctuating answer amused her a little. "I thought multiple choices were only for exams. Am I supposed to pick an answer from the above three?" she asked him.

Sebastian shook his head. He needed to go before he made a complete fool of himself.

"I was leaving," he confirmed, nodding toward the door behind her. "For some reason, my attending this reunion seemed to mean a great deal to my mother, so I told her that I would go. But I'm *really* not comfortable here." He looked around at the sea of mostly unfamiliar faces. "Being here kind of feels like putting on a sweater that used to fit but doesn't anymore."

"Because you've outgrown it."

It wasn't a question. She knew exactly what he was saying, because he'd described exactly the way she felt about attending this reunion.

Rather than nostalgia, what she'd heard in the various conversations she'd either taken in or overheard was the longing of former gridiron stars and ex-cheerleaders talking about the past, the scene of their glory days. For most it had been downhill after that. Hearing them talk just made her sad.

"My father made me come," she admitted.

"Your father," he echoed. That was right—he remembered his mother saying something about the old man's miraculous recovery. His mother insisted the miracle came in the form of Brianna. "How is he? I heard he made a full recovery, thanks to you."

She could feel color creeping up to her cheeks. Brianna quickly shrugged away his take on the story. "I don't know how much I really had to do with it, but my father did recover and he's doing just fine. Thanks for asking."

There were a thousand things to ask—and nothing left to talk about. He needed to go before the situation grew any more awkward. "Well, tell him I said hi."

"I will." She reciprocated and told him, "Say hi to your mom for me."

She'd always liked his mother a great deal, but after Sebastian had left her life, she couldn't make herself remain in contact with the woman. Being around Barbara Hunter reminded her far too much of what she had ultimately lost.

"Will do," he answered. "Well, I guess I'll see you around, Bree." He had no idea why he'd just said that, since he would be leaving for Japan soon.

"See you around," she echoed with a quick nod of her head.

"Well, what do we have here? Sebastian Hunter and Brianna MacKenzie, the king and queen of prom, together again!" Tiffany Riley, the official reunion coordinator, gushed ecstatically as she came up to them.

Chapter Three

Before she had a chance to recover from Tiffany's suddenly popping up, or to come up with a polite way to deny that they were "together," Brianna found herself being abruptly ushered to the center of the room, as was Sebastian. He seemed just as stunned by the former head cheerleader as Brianna was.

Aided by the element of surprise, Tiffany had brought them both over to stand before the band. The five-man group appeared to wait for some sort of signal from the woman.

In a voice loud enough to be heard not just across the populated gym but all the way across the street as well, Tiffany continued doing what she had always done best: talking and manipulating.

"Hey, everyone, what d'you say we get our king and

queen of the prom to re-create that last magical dance
for us?"

She definitely did *not* want to go there, Brianna
thought.

Especially not with everyone staring at them. It stirred
up too many memories, too many feelings. Memories
and feelings she wasn't sure she would be able to contain once aroused.

She slanted a look at Tiffany, who had a very smug
expression on her face. Why? In high school, Tiffany
had done everything she could to try to win Sebastian
back. He'd dated the blonde cheerleader before he'd
become *her* boyfriend, Brianna recalled, and although
he'd once told her that he'd never considered himself
and Tiffany to be a couple, Tiffany obviously had.

So why was Tiffany bringing attention to them now?
Brianna wondered, feeling decidedly uncomfortable.
This made no sense.

"No, I really don't thin—" Brianna began to beg off.

"I haven't danced since—"

Sebastian's voice blended with hers, but it was as if
neither one of them had spoken, for all the effect it had
on Tiffany. She apparently had decided to turn a deaf
ear to both of them, focusing only on getting them to
dance.

For just the slightest second, a smirk crossed Tiffany's
full lips. She was enjoying their discomfort, Brianna realized. *Still hateful after all these years.*

"Aw, they're shy. Looks like they need some en-
couragement," Tiffany mocked. "Okay, give it up for

Sebastian and Brianna," she cried, beckoning for the attendees to applaud or chant the couple's names. Or better yet, both. The crowd complied immediately.

Tiffany's smirk turned into a look of satisfaction. "Music, please, boys," she called out to the band, then tossed a final, somewhat condescending bone to the audience. "And, for those of you who don't remember, that last 'magical' song they danced to was Etta James's 'At Last.'"

Tiffany, a commando in bright lavender taffeta, narrowed her eyes as she appraised the couple she had hustled to the center of the dance floor. The look on her face seemed to say, "So, what are you waiting for?"

Sebastian was far from happy about this turn of events, but the last thing he wanted was to cause a scene. The thought that no good deed went unpunished crossed his mind. If he hadn't come here to please his mother, he wouldn't be going through this now.

"Tiffany's going to bully us into dancing to that song. You realize that, don't you?" Sebastian whispered to Brianna, barely moving his lips.

Brianna did her best not to shiver as his breath slid along her bare shoulder. A wealth of old, repressed sensations and feelings came cascading down on her before she had a chance to block them again.

She focused only on what Sebastian had just said, not on what she'd just felt. "Bullying comes naturally to Tiffany," Brianna whispered back, recalling several instances during her high school years. Tiffany had always been obsessed with holding court and being the center of attention. The cheerleader had been utterly furious when she'd lost the bid to be crowned prom queen, especially to someone who hadn't lobbied to win the title.

Despite the fact that, the whole time she'd been driving here, she'd done her best to anesthetize herself against Sebastian should she run into him, she could feel that old thrill trying to break through.

It had just about succeeded when Sebastian suddenly took her hand and said, "One dance can't hurt."

A lot you know, she thought grudgingly. *Nobody broke your heart the way you broke mine.*

Brianna pressed her lips together to keep the words back. If she was lucky, they'd have this dance and then he'd leave.

If you're luckier, you'll have this dance and he won't leave.

The thought startled her.

Out loud she said, "Guess not," as she forced herself to smile broadly up into his face—strictly for appearances' sake.

The strains of the classic song filled the carefully decorated gym. The next moment, someone had the bright idea to dim the lights. And just like that, Brianna felt herself being teleported back across time and space until she was right there, at the prom, with the last song surrounding her like a soft, warm wrap.

Before she realized it, or could do anything to prevent it, her body was blending together with Sebastian's.

Just as it had that night.

The whole world had been at her feet that night. Everything had been fresh and new and it had whispered the promise of such wonderful things to come.

As it had turned out, it was the last time that she had felt sure of anything. The last time she'd felt secure. It had been just hours before her entire world was upended. While she was dancing with Sebastian, her father had been involved in that awful car accident, when an underage driver had jumped the light and plowed right into him.

Her whole life had changed in a matter of seconds. Instead of going away to college with Sebastian and beginning a new chapter in her life, not only going away to college but also moving in with Sebastian, she'd opted to remain home and help her father recover from the accident.

She'd thought her heart would literally break as she watched Sebastian leave, even though she had been the one to encourage him to go.

Was that really all those years ago? she wondered now. It seemed like just yesterday, especially with all these old feelings ambushing her.

Maybe her father was right. Maybe she really did need to take a short break from everything. From constantly shouldering problems that weren't always just her own. Her ability to empathize helped her be the kind of nurse every patient wanted, but at times it wreaked havoc with her own life, continually draining her.

So just for tonight, she decided abruptly, she was going to allow herself to reminisce, to go back to a time when she'd believed that her life was going to be absolutely nothing short of perfect.

"You still wear that perfume."

Sebastian's voice, low and still incredibly—and unintentionally—sensual, crept into her consciousness, catching her off guard.

It took her a second to play back the words and understand them. It took her another second to realize that she'd laid her head on his shoulder.

The way she had that last night.

Blinking, Brianna raised her head and looked at him. "What?"

"Your perfume," he repeated. "It's the same one you wore that night." He remembered how it had eroded any defenses he might have had and had made him want her in the worst way.

"It's the same one I wear all the time. I guess I'm not very exciting," she confessed with a slight, careless shrug.

Exciting or not, she was still her own person. Her own person who was committed to going her own way whenever she had to and helping others whenever she could. Being a nurse wasn't just what she did—it was what she *was*.

"Oh, I wouldn't exactly say that," Sebastian told her.

Maybe it was the combination of the perfume, the song and the fact that, for the most part, he'd led a fairly solitary life overseas. There were more than a few times when he'd felt alone in the crowd for these past few years, despite living in one of the most crowded cities in Japan.

Whatever the reason, holding Brianna like this, having her perfume fill his senses, managed to stir up some old, treasured memories. Memories that nonetheless felt a little misty, because time had a way of creating holes in the fabric of life as it began to stretch out.

The memories allowed him to suddenly feel as if he had been transported back to the past. To the last time he'd held Brianna in his arms. Then his head had been full of dreams for both of them.

He'd made love to her for the first—and only—time that night.

The wave of nostalgia that hit him was almost overpoweringly strong.

Brianna was undergoing a struggle of her own—and losing.

Talk, damn it. Say something. Something vague and neutral. Before you wind up making a fool of yourself and melting all over him.

Desperate, Brianna hit on the only topic she could actually think of. "So, how is your mother doing these days?"

"Not as well as I'd like," Sebastian admitted in an unguarded moment.

Ordinarily, he wasn't given to voicing his concerns or feelings. The years had made him far more stoic than he had been.

Less than five minutes in Brianna's company and he was regressing, he thought, annoyed with himself.

The concern he saw entering her eyes surprised him. "What do you mean by that?"

A simple excuse occurred to him. One that was, ultimately, a lie. But he had never been able to lie to Brianna. To start now just seemed wrong.

So he told her the truth. "The doctor said she'd had a minor stroke—reminded me just how fragile life really is. I was planning on having a lengthy visit with her over the Christmas holidays, but once she told me about her condition, I rearranged my vacation plans and flew out as soon as possible."

He paused for a moment, debating his next words. It exposed his vulnerable side, but then, this was Brianna, whom he had once trusted implicitly. He supposed, simply because old habits were hard to break, part of him still did.

"Mom made me realize that putting off the visit home might not be the wisest thing to do. If something had happened to her before I got a chance to see her, I'd never forgive myself."

She knew he wasn't being dramatic. His mother was a wonderful woman whom everyone absolutely loved. Including Sebastian. And her.

"So here I am," Sebastian concluded.

The wheels in her head had instantly begun turning at the first mention of his mother's illness. The nurse in her was never off duty.

"Has your mother ever had a stroke before?"

"No, not to my knowledge." He came back at her with his own question. "Why?"

Her shoulders rose and then fell in a casual shrug. "No real reason. I'm just trying to pull some facts together."

He'd been so caught up in the moment—and trying not to be—that he'd completely forgotten. "That's right. You became a nurse, didn't you?"

Brianna nodded. "After my father got well, there was this tremendous feeling of relief. But at the same time, there was also this feeling of 'what do I do with myself now?'"

"The words 'relax a little' come to mind," he told her.

She smiled as she shook her head. "Not really in my nature. Besides, going into nursing seemed like the natural progression at the time. I like helping people, like getting them motivated and helping them realize that the only thing holding them back from achieving their goals—no matter what those goals are—is themselves."

Sebastian had grown quiet and there was a strange look on his face now.

She flushed a little ruefully. "I'm talking too much, aren't I?"

She was even prettier than she had been when he'd left, he thought now. Her looks were enhanced by a confidence that hadn't been there when they'd gone together.

He found himself having to struggle to keep from being drawn in.

"I don't think so," he answered honestly. Who would have thought that the feelings he had for her were still there? That they hadn't disappeared but had just gone into hibernation? "When my mother asked me to attend this reunion—"

"She *asked* you to attend?" Brianna echoed in surprise. That sounded so much like what her father had done, she was struck by the odd similarity.

He nodded. "My coming to the reunion seemed to mean a lot to her. Why is beyond me," he admitted. But then, the workings of a female mind mystified him. "What?" he asked when he saw her mouth beginning to curve. To his knowledge, he hadn't said anything funny.

"Don't act as if you came here kicking and screaming," she told him, amused at his protest. "The Sebastian I remember never did anything he didn't want to do."

The shrug was careless, even though he didn't take his eyes off her for a second.

"Maybe I've gotten more thoughtful in my old age," he speculated.

"Twenty-nine only qualifies for old age if you happen to be related to a fruit fly," she countered.

Sebastian smiled in response, a slightly self-deprecating expression on his face. She'd forgotten how easily that could get to her. Several more couples had joined them on the dance floor, so it no longer felt as if the two of them were putting on an exhibition strictly for Tiffany's amusement.

When Sebastian stopped moving about on the floor a moment later, she looked up at him curiously. "Why did you stop dancing?"

"Because the music stopped playing," he answered simply.

Damn it, how could she have missed that? Had she

been *that* mesmerized by him? That couldn't be allowed to happen.

"Right." Embarrassed, Brianna stepped back, dropping her hands from his. "Well, I guess we've fulfilled any leftover obligations from that last prom."

At least the obligations to strangers, she couldn't help thinking.

"Oh, no, you two aren't planning on ditching us already, are you?" Tiffany gushed, suddenly coming up to them again. "Maybe for a little secret rendezvous?" she asked with a laugh that threatened to turn Brianna's stomach.

Like an unwanted guest who was oblivious to any attempt to get her to leave, Tiffany hooked one arm through each of theirs, placing herself strategically between them. Her smile was as fake as it was wide.

"Is that it?" she pressed. "Do you two *really* intend to make up for lost time?"

He knew that telling Tiffany it was none of her business just made her more curious—and more determined to prove that she was right.

So he deftly avoided a direct answer. "I guess I can stay for a little longer," Sebastian told the former cheerleader.

Without meaning to or being totally conscious of doing it, he glanced in Brianna's direction to see if she'd been persuaded to remain for a while longer as well.

Or, he supposed, strong-armed into it.

He had to admit that he expected to see fireworks between the two women at any second. His money was on Brianna. Of the two, she appeared to be in far better shape—not to mention a lot feistier than Tiffany.

"Wonderful," Tiffany exclaimed, clapping her hands together. In what seemed like an afterthought, she looked in Brianna's direction. "And you, Bree?"

There had always been something condescending in her voice, Brianna thought, no matter whom she addressed. It used to intimidate her, but she'd had to shoulder so much in these past few years that the snide attitude of one small-minded woman no longer bothered her in the slightest, the way it might have at some other time.

She supposed that, as Sebastian had already said, it would do no harm to hang around here a little longer. After all, after tonight he would most likely go back to his work, which she'd heard was out of the country, and she would go back to hers. And their paths would never cross again.

So she awarded Tiffany with a carefree smile and said, "Sure, why not?"

"Great." This time, because they both seemed so willing, the word sounded a little less than upbeat. "This way, please," Tiffany told them, leading them to another part of the gym.

Sebastian stayed where he was for a moment longer and asked, "And just what's 'this way'?"

It was obvious to both of them that Tiffany didn't like being questioned or having to explain herself. She was, as Brianna would later tell her father when he asked how things had gone, a control freak in search of her own country to rule.

"Why, a photographer, you distrustful man." Tiffany laughed as if she had just said something exceedingly witty. "We're trying to put together an album of former students. You know, kind of like a 'where are they now?' sort of thing."

Sebastian looked at Brianna and asked, "You okay with that?" The display of concern toward Brianna irritated Tiffany no end, even as she continued maintaining her completely artificial smile.

"Sure," Brianna agreed. "I've got no problem having my picture taken."

"Thank you." Tiffany's gushing tone had been abandoned. What lay beneath had definite touches of frost to it, as did the glance she shot Brianna's way.

But the next moment, Tiffany once again reclaimed center stage and wound her expensively manicured fingers around the microphone, and the wide, shallow smile had returned.

"Attention. Can I have your attention?" she requested in a voice that grew louder with each passing syllable. "The photographer's been making the rounds to your tables, but now it's time for all of us to stand up and come together for group shots," she announced. "We all thought it might be fun if we did it the way the yearbook was done—pictures taken in our old clubs. Those of you, like myself—" unable to stop herself, she allowed the superior smirk to pass over her face again "—who belonged to an endless number of groups will be forced to have your picture taken in each and every one of them. Just remember, this is ultimately for the good of the student body."

"Is she for real?" Sebastian whispered the question to Brianna. He'd turned his head away at the last moment so that Tiffany wouldn't be able to overhear him.

Brianna took a quick survey of the woman at the microphone. As far as "real" went, she highly doubted it. Tiffany had obviously had her nose shortened, her chin reinforced, not to mention that her cup size had been increased by a multiple of two. Her hair was neither her natural color, nor, from what she remembered, actually hers. Her hairdo was comprised of elaborately woven extensions.

"Not as far as I can tell," Brianna quipped.

Sebastian suddenly had to bite his lower lip to keep from laughing.

Brianna saw the contained laughter in his eyes when he looked at her and that old feeling, the one she was desperately struggling to block, rose up and found her again.

She reminded herself that this was an isolated evening, one with ties to the past and absolutely no ties to either one of their futures.

With that understood and taken into consideration, she allowed herself to react to him, but only as long as she kept in mind that all her tomorrows would be without him, just as so many of her yesterdays had been.

Tiffany beckoned over the photographer, a tall, balding man who had a camera hanging from his neck and another one held firmly in his hands.

"All right, Alan, let the snapping begin," Tiffany declared as she turned her body three-quarters toward the photographer, her hands on her hips and her head thrown back.

She was posing for him.

To her chagrin, the photographer turned his camera toward Sebastian and Brianna and began shooting shot after shot.

Tiffany collected herself and stormed away.

Chapter Four

"I think you've got more than enough photographs now."

Something in Sebastian's voice must have told the photographer there was no room for argument. Resigned, the man nodded and lowered the camera that he had been firing at them in rapid fashion.

"Yeah, I guess maybe I do," the photographer murmured.

The next moment, he was turning his attention toward other alumni, his camera once again shooting.

Sebastian became acutely aware of Brianna beside him and the silence that seemed to seal them into their own private bubble, despite all the people and noise around them.

"I guess I should have asked you before sending that guy away," Sebastian said.

For old times' sake, Brianna decided to absolve him of any guilt, especially since, unlike Tiffany, she had absolutely no desire to be digitally captured and immortalized pretending she was still a teenager.

"He was getting on my nerves, too," she confided to Sebastian.

"Good to know," he murmured, feeling more awkward and at loose ends than he could recall feeling since…well, since more than ten years ago when he'd initially walked up to her and struck up a conversation. At the time, he'd tried hard not to trip over his own tongue because he thought she was just so genuinely pretty, without resorting to any of the usual enhancing beauty aids that the other girls used.

He took a long breath. This was the part where he took his leave. He'd say a few vague, noncommittal words, something generic and nonspecific about it being nice to see her again, or it was fun catching up, and then he'd get the hell out of there as fast as he could.

The fact that they hadn't caught up wasn't really supposed to matter.

Except that it did.

This was the girl he'd left behind, the one who "got away," as his mother had told him more than once over the past ten years.

Not that Brianna had made a single move that took her out of his reach.

No, *he* was the one who had made all the moves. *He*

was the one who had left Bedford alone after they had initially made plans to leave together.

But the plans that he could have sworn had been written in stone turned out to have been written in tapioca pudding. He had gone on to the college that had accepted them both, while Brianna had staunchly remained at home, nursing her father back from the jaws of paralysis to become the healed man he was today.

In a word, she had just continued being Brianna.

And now he was here, trying to collect himself after just having held in his arms the only woman, if he were being truly honest, who had ever mattered to him in that all-important way.

And, yes, damn it, he was experiencing regrets. Very real regrets. Something he'd *thought* he was finally beyond having. He was an intelligent, successful man and that meant he'd moved on.

Or at least he'd *thought* he'd moved on.

Except that now he wasn't so sure. "Moving on" didn't have the painful, gut-twisting feeling attached to it, the one he was experiencing now.

Did it?

And, if he'd genuinely moved on, he wouldn't have heard himself saying this little gem: "Listen, would you like to go get a drink somewhere, or maybe go out to dinner sometime? I'm in town for at least another week...."

Abruptly running out of steam, Sebastian let his voice trail off.

Another week. Seven days, and then he'd be gone

again. He would be here just long enough to rip open all her old wounds and then he'd go again, his job here done.

Say no, Bree. For God's sake, save yourself and say no.

Her problem was that she never listened to that little, all-important inner voice, the one that always made such sense.

The one that had urged her, ten years ago, to go on with her life. To hire someone if she could for her father and get her degree the way she'd planned for years, instead of standing there with tears in her eyes, telling Sebastian that she couldn't just leave her father with strangers.

That same lack of common sense—as well as lack of self-preservation—now had her saying to Sebastian, "That would be nice." It was a phrase that opened up the door to a world of possibilities she *knew* she wasn't emotionally equipped to deal with at this point.

Too late now.

"How about tomorrow night?" Sebastian asked, even as he told himself that what he was actually supposed to say at this point was "Good. I'll call you," or even "Great. I'll get back to you about details." And then leave it at that.

The *last* thing he was supposed to do was get specific. And citing a date like tomorrow didn't give his common sense enough time to kick in and talk him out of this extremely rash move.

Why am I nodding? her little voice demanded.

Worse, she thought, why was she asking Sebastian, "Is six good for you?"

Six is terrible for me. I misspoke. How about we change that from tomorrow to the twelfth of never?

The handful of lifesaving words raged in Sebastian's head, helplessly caged and unable to break free in order to slip off his tongue.

So instead, what he heard was his own doom being sealed, his death knell sounding as he responded—rather than saying, "No, no, a thousand times no"—"Perfect."

"All right, then I'll expect you at six tomorrow."

"What's your address?" Sebastian asked, piercing a hole in the rubber balloon of her desperate thoughts.

Brianna blinked as she looked at him, her mind a sudden blank. "What?"

"Your address," he specified. When she still looked at him as if he was using a foreign language, he added, "So I can come and pick you up."

The fog lifted. "Right." The smile she flashed at him was bordering on anemic. "I still live in the same house," Brianna told him. "Never had the time to move out," she added.

The smile he saw on her lips was fast—but lethal nonetheless.

Just as lethal, he realized, as it ever was.

Perhaps even more.

Time had been very good to her. The pretty little high school senior was now a strikingly beautiful woman.

"That'll make it easy for me to find." As he stood

there, drawing out the conversation when he knew he should be running for cover, he had a sudden, strong and nearly irresistible urge to kiss her, despite the fact that approximately half their graduating class was milling around to bear witness to his insanity.

He called himself seven kinds of a fool. It was enough—for now—to stop him.

"I'll walk you to your car," he finally heard himself volunteer.

Panic vied with a surge of pulsating excitement. "You're leaving, too?" she asked.

He nodded, glancing over his shoulder. He spotted the former cheerleader looking their way. "Thought I should make good my getaway before Tiffany comes up with something else."

Brianna nodded. "Tiffany's married to a doctor now. Well, a dentist," she corrected, not because she thought of one career as being superior to the other but because she wanted to be accurate. "Actually, it's rather lucky he is a dentist." Sebastian raised a quizzical eyebrow, waiting for an explanation. "They have three kids and all three are in braces. When they smile on a sunny day, the glare could blind you."

Brianna heard him laugh at that and found the low, sensual sound oddly comforting. She tried to persuade herself that his reaction one way or another didn't matter to her.

She reminded herself that she had come a long way since she'd been that heartbroken, starry-eyed girl who'd cried into her pillow every night for a month.

Right now, though, none of that could get her to change the way she was responding to him. Couldn't erase the warm glow growing inside her, created by his nearness.

He'd always had that sort of effect on her, she recalled.

"She never forgave you for dumping her, you know," she told Sebastian.

The protest was automatic—and with feeling. "I didn't dump her."

She was only telling him what she knew that Tiffany believed. "I think it felt that way to her."

He wanted to correct the record, strictly for old times' sake, he silently insisted, not because it mattered to him to be blameless in her eyes.

"To dump someone, you have to be going with that person to begin with," he reminded her. "And we weren't going together."

"She certainly thought that you were going together," Brianna dutifully pointed out, recalling the vicious looks she'd been subjected to by Tiffany and her circle of friends.

They had begun walking toward the exit and he found himself quickening his pace just a little. The conversation wasn't on a path he wanted to take.

"I can't help what she thought. I just know that it wasn't anything I said to her—or even alluded to. To be honest," he continued as they walked out of the gym and down the empty, dimly lit hallway, "Tiffany kind of scared me."

He was kidding, right? "She weighed all of ninety-eight pounds to your one-eighty." Brianna knew that, because back then Tiffany was forever bragging about losing weight and hardly ever allowed herself to eat anything of substance.

"Her weight had nothing to do with it," he maintained. "A stick of dynamite can blow up a barn. And irrational people are capable of doing some really very scary, unhinged things.

"Where's your car?" Sebastian asked, abruptly changing the subject.

The last thing he wanted to do was talk about Tiffany and the past. He didn't really want to dwell on the past at all, because if he allowed himself to do that, then he would start to remember just how much he'd once loved Brianna and how irrationally hurt and cheated he'd felt when he was made to choose—not in so many words but in actual fact—between the woman he loved and going on to pursue his dreams.

Brianna was supposed to have been part of those dreams, not an alternative choice.

But looking back now, he couldn't help but wonder, if only for a brief, unguarded moment, if his choice had been the right one.

Sure it was. Don't start second-guessing yourself. You see? This is why you should never have come back to Bedford.

Except that he had to and he knew it. To willfully not come back when his mother had made it so clear that she needed him would have been, if nothing else, in-

credibly selfish on his part. And that didn't even begin
to take into consideration the fact that if something had
actually happened to his mother, he would have never
forgiven himself for not seeing her one last time.

Especially since she'd made a point of requesting it.

It was that moment, as this thought began to sink
deep into his mind, when for the very first time he actually understood just what Brianna must have gone
through all those years ago. Understood how she felt
when her father had survived the accident but had been
given the prognosis that he would never walk again,
never function independently in any manner, shape or
form.

Never be the man he had been until that terrible accident.

Now he understood how very torn she had to have
been between following her conscience, which bound
her to the man who had done everything to give her
the very best possible life, and following her heart and
going away to college with him.

Sebastian looked at her and, before he could think
to stop himself, he heard himself saying to her, "Bree,
I'm sorry."

They were out in the parking lot now, walking toward the spot where Brianna had parked her car. His
words, coming completely out of the blue and cocooned
in such heart-wrenching sadness, left her utterly confused.

She needed an explanation. "Sorry about what?"

By then Sebastian's instincts of self-preservation had

finally kicked in, the same ones that told him there was no purpose in revisiting the past.

They supplied the right words to get him out of this verbal grave he had managed, so quickly, to dig for himself.

"Sorry if I was a bit rusty back there. You know, on the dance floor," he added, knowing this had to be up for an award somewhere as one of the lamest excuses of the decade, if not the century. "It's been a while since I've done any dancing."

She had a hunch that wasn't what Sebastian had initially alluded to with his apology, but she just couldn't see the point of making him twist and turn in the wind.

What on earth for?

So instead, she just shrugged it off and said something equally bland.

"Really? I would have never known. Not that I'm exactly a double threat on the dance floor myself, but you seemed pretty smooth to me back there."

To be honest, having him hold her in his arms had effectively destroyed the ability on her part to take notice of *anything* else.

Sebastian laughed softly under his breath, another group of memories popping out of hiding and scampering lightly across his brain in toe shoes.

And then he smiled at her. "You never did find fault with me, even when I said it was okay to, did you, Brianna?"

She shrugged again, the movement more deliberate than careless.

"Life's too short to nitpick," Brianna answered. Suddenly aware of where she was in the parking lot, she stopped walking. She'd almost walked right past her vehicle. "Well, this is my car, so your escort service is no longer needed."

Nice going, Bree. Could you be more awkward sounding? she upbraided herself. She was never an out-and-out wit, but she also never sounded as if her tongue didn't quite work right, either.

His attention drawn to her car, Sebastian looked at the light blue vehicle and recognition set in. "Hey, isn't that—?"

"Yes," Brianna answered, anticipating what he was about to ask. "It's the old Toyota my dad gave me as an early graduation present just before the prom." At the last minute, she'd decided to leave J.T.'s CR-V behind and drive this car instead. It seemed more in keeping with the evening's whole nostalgic mood. "It still runs like a dream—well, close to a dream, anyway," she amended with a nervous little laugh. "But I really don't see the need to get rid of it just because it's an old model and the paint could use a little freshening.

"I guess I just tend to stick with things," she added.

Too late she realized what that might have sounded like to Sebastian: a rebuke for choosing to move on, to shed the city he'd been born and raised in.

The city where she had remained.

Pressing her lips together, Brianna searched for the right words to help her fix what she'd just done.

When none occurred to her, Brianna fell back on a

tried-and-true excuse. "But that's just me, I guess. Just an old stick-in-the-mud."

"Old sticks never looked so good," Sebastian murmured with appreciation before his mind had a chance to filter his words.

He was developing a serious case of foot-in-mouth disease, he upbraided himself.

Sebastian stood back as she unlocked her car door on the driver's side. Then, reaching past her, he opened it and held the door open for her as she slid in.

The skirt of Brianna's street-length dress rose up on one side, climbing up rather high on her thigh before she had a chance to pull it down again.

She still had the best legs he'd ever seen, Sebastian caught himself thinking.

Some things, fortunately, never changed.

And then he forced himself to focus on making his final getaway. "Okay, then. Tomorrow at six. Your place, right?"

"Right."

She had no one to blame but herself, Brianna thought. She knew she could still change her mind, still act on the second thoughts that she was now experiencing at a prodigious rate. Act on them and come up with some kind of an excuse.

Plausible or not, Sebastian would have to accept whatever rationale she gave him. After all, he couldn't exactly *force* her to come to dinner with him, now, could he?

Of course not.

Brianna was still thinking this as she drove away, watching Sebastian get smaller and smaller in her rear-view mirror.

Chapter Five

With a sigh, Brianna stepped out of the latest dress she'd just tried on and tossed it onto the growing mountain of fabric on her bed.

Why didn't anything look right on her?

This was getting serious. Her frustration doubled and grew by the nanosecond.

When she'd pulled back the sliding mirrored door of her wardrobe in her bedroom, approximately forty-five minutes ago, Brianna was fairly certain she knew exactly what she was going to wear to this dinner, which she should have never agreed to. But once she had put the dress on, it just looked all wrong, so she had gone on to choice number two and put *that* on.

It met the same fate.

As did choices number three through five.

And, at the same time, with each discarded garment, the butterflies in her stomach multiplied.

Exasperated when yet another choice seemed woefully inadequate on her, several disparaging, less-than-flattering words rose to her lips, poised for release. But she remained silent when she saw Carrie curiously stick her head into her room.

The old soul trapped in a child's body looked at the ever-growing pile of clothes that had accumulated on Brianna's double bed. After a moment, the blue eyes shifted from the bed to her.

"Why are all the clothes out, Mama? Are you cleaning?"

"No, honey. I just can't find anything to wear," Brianna answered, doing her best not to allow the growing despair to surface in her voice.

Why had she ever agreed to this? And why hadn't she noticed before tonight that *nothing* she owned fit her the way it was supposed to?

Her response confused her ordinarily unflappable daughter. Carrie gestured toward the bed. "Sure you can, Mama. It's all right there, on your bed. *Lots* of clothes," she emphasized.

Ever the practical child, Brianna thought with affection.

"What I mean is that everything I tried on just wasn't... pretty enough," she concluded, finally settling on the right word to describe her dissatisfaction.

"Clothes aren't pretty, Mama," said Carrie, the picture of endearing innocence. "You are," she insisted definitively.

The child should be bottled as a tranquilizing agent. "You're right—clothes *aren't* pretty." In the back of her mind, she wondered if she should be recording this conversation, saving it to replay when her tiny soul-of-logic turned into a sullen, typical teenager experiencing out-of-control angst over having a wardrobe that was too dull, too boring or just plain no longer sufficient for her current needs.

Brianna took a deep breath, trying her best to center herself. Maybe the solution to her problem was just to let a neutral bystander pick her outfit.

She glanced down at her daughter. "All right, what would *you* pick out to wear if you were going out to eat with someone who had once been very special to you but who you haven't really seen in the last ten years?"

Rather than dive into the piles of clothing strewn all over her mother's bed, Carrie turned toward her with a question of her own. "Why didn't you see the special person? Was he hiding?"

Maybe. Maybe I was, too, Brianna thought. Hiding from the pain, from the fact that her heart felt as if it had been literally broken in two. Someone you loved was supposed to support you during a crisis, not go on with his own life and ignore what you were going through.

"He went away to college," she told Carrie.

Carrie looked at her with wide, caring eyes. "And you couldn't go?"

How was it that this child could always strip everything down to its bare essentials, making the situation appear so simple, so cut-and-dried, even when it didn't feel that way?

"Grandpa was in a big accident—before you were born," she qualified when she saw the question rising in her daughter's intense blue eyes, "and I had to take care of him."

Carrie nodded her head. The little girl was probably merely taking in her words, but it almost felt as if Carrie was giving Brianna her own seal of approval for what she'd done.

"And he's all better now," Carrie noted with no small pleasure. She beamed at the only woman she had ever known to be her mother. "You did a good job taking care of him, Mama."

Brianna returned her daughter's smile, feeling heartened. Everything always seemed better, brighter, more hopeful whenever Carrie was around.

"I did, didn't I?" For some unknown reason, Brianna felt better now and was more confident.

Grateful, she kissed the top of Carrie's head. There were times when she couldn't help wondering exactly who was taking care of whom.

What she *did* know in her heart was that she would be utterly and completely *lost* without this unassuming girl.

"Okay, Carrie, you tell me. Which dress should I wear?"

This time Carrie *did* turn her attention to the clothes

haphazardly heaped on the bed, a thoughtful expression wrinkling her small brow as she studied the dresses.

After a moment, Carrie walked around the bed like a half-pint judge at a county fair pie bake-off contest, slowly regarding each "contestant" she viewed before her. Once or twice, she touched an article of clothing until, digging through the tallest mountain, her slender, small fingers closed over a scrap of bright blue fabric.

Pulling on it, Carrie managed to draw out a simple dress that had been thrown onto the pile without the benefit of having been tried on. Brianna remembered dismissing the garment out of hand as being just too plain.

Carrie held it up for her now. "This one," the child pronounced.

Brianna regarded her daughter's choice. "That one? You're sure?"

Carrie nodded her head enthusiastically. Still, the dress didn't really spark her imagination, so Brianna reached for another, far more formal, dress.

"How about…?"

She never got any further, because Carrie just moved her head from side to side, summarily vetoing the new choice.

Instead, she deliberately separated the dress she'd selected from the others and now held it up for her review.

"Try it on, Mama," she coaxed.

With a shrug, Brianna slipped the dress on, wiggling into the soft, short skirt and allowing it to glide lovingly over her hips. With short, focused movements, she smoothed down the fabric.

The moment the dress was on her, Carrie's smile grew wider. "You look really beautiful, Mama," she declared with satisfied finality.

How could she bring herself to argue with that? Brianna wondered fondly.

"Well, if you really like it that much, then I'll *have* to wear it," she told the little girl. Maybe it wasn't all *that* bad.

Just then, after rapping once sharply on the unlocked door, Brianna's father peered in.

"You ready yet?" he asked with just a touch of impatience in his voice.

She was just freshening up her makeup. "Just about, Dad."

Jim MacKenzie shook his head in absolute, mystified wonder.

"I swear, it took less time for Michelangelo to paint the Sistine Chapel ceiling than it does for an ordinary woman to get ready," he mumbled under his breath— but it was still audible. "Your mother, God rest her soul, was just the same way," he admitted, allowing a fond note to slip into his voice. "She started getting ready on a Thursday for a party she was attending the following Saturday."

"We take a long time because we want to look good," Carrie piped up.

Her father did his best not to laugh out loud, while

Brianna declared, "What she said," with complete approval.

Jim shifted his eyes to look at his daughter. "Well, I guess it would be worth his wait—if this guy were waiting in our living room for you," he added with a smile.

Startled, Brianna glanced at her watch, then at her father. She'd lost track of time and it was getting late. "He's not, is he?"

"Nope. By my calculation, he's got about ten more minutes. Unless he believes in being early—" As if on cue, the doorbell rang. Amused, Jim nodded. "Speak of the devil." With that, Brianna's father stepped back into the hall. "I'd better go let him in before he thinks you've stood him up."

Maybe it would be better that way, Brianna thought as the tsunami in her stomach rose to a record-breaking height. For now she kept that to herself.

Glancing over to where Carrie had been just a second ago dispensing her little-old-lady wisdom, Brianna realized that the girl was no longer there. She had just *too* much energy.

"Where's Carrie?" she asked, turning toward her father.

As if caught off guard by the question, he looked over toward the corner where he'd last seen her.

Pointing, he told her, "She was just right here—" And then he sighed. The girl had more moves than three-week-old puppies. "Probably answering the door," he realized. Carrie was *nothing* if not a challenge to keep track of. And he knew that with each passing year, it was only going to get worse. He sighed now, as if mentally bracing himself. "Don't worry, I'll go get her."

"No, we'll *both* go get her," Brianna said, grabbing her shoes in her hand rather than pausing to put them on. Right now, her temper was at the end of a dangerously short fuse. "I told her a hundred times she wasn't to open the door by herself."

She was such a smart little girl in all other ways— why did she insist on disregarding this most important of rules?

Okay, they lived in a very safe neighborhood, but that didn't mean that someone who was less than trustworthy couldn't just come in at will and ruin their lives by abducting Carrie—or worse.

At that exact moment, Carrie had reached the front door and was presently yanking it open. The door was not unduly heavy, but neither was it light, and the determined girl had to use both hands to budge the front door from its frame.

"Hi," she declared brightly upon achieving success. She was visibly checking out the person standing on the other side of her doorstep.

Expecting to see someone near his own height, or thereabouts, Sebastian had to lower his eyes before saying, "Hi. Is Brianna around?"

After appraising him, the little girl nodded. Then, turning her head ever so slightly so that her voice would carry inside the house, Carrie raised her volume and called out, "That guy is here to see you, Mama."

Mama?

The simple, two-syllable word completely knocked the pins right out from under Sebastian.

When he'd seen her again last night after such a long absence of contact, it really hadn't occurred to him that Brianna had gotten married, much less that she'd had a child.

"She's your mother?" he heard himself asking the child as he struggled to keep his voice steady and lofty sounding.

Even to his own untrained ear, Sebastian was forced to admit that he hadn't exactly succeeded.

"Uh-huh." Large, luminous blue eyes regarded him. "Are you the guy my mama thinks is special?" she asked.

The question took him completely aback and more than a little by surprise.

Special?

Did Brianna really think he was special, after all this time had passed? Or had the very pretty little girl with the rosebud mouth just gotten her facts rather confused?

"I really don't know," Sebastian replied quite honestly.

Before he had to face answering any more questions from the pint-size interrogator, he saw Brianna hurrying in, looking equal parts flustered and absolutely gorgeous. And she was headed for the girl.

"Carrie, what did I tell you about opening the door when you're alone?" she demanded.

"Not to," the little girl replied dutifully. "But I'm not alone," she protested in the next breath. "You and Grandpa are here."

"But we're not close enough," Brianna reminded her.

Carrie cocked her head. "For what, Mama?"

"We're not close enough to stop someone if they wanted to grab you and take you along with them."

In utterly logical fashion, Carrie glanced up at Sebastian. "You didn't want to take me with you, did you?" she asked Sebastian.

"I'm here to take out Brianna—your mom," he tagged on.

And why would she have agreed to see him, to go out for dinner, if she was a married woman?

Unless...

He looked at Brianna. "Is she yours?" he asked. He already knew the answer to that, or thought he did. He was trying to create a starting point for himself and then go from there.

Brianna smiled, one arm going around the slender child and pulling her closer.

"She is that," she acknowledged both fondly and firmly.

"Hello, son," her father said heartily, coming in behind his daughter and addressing the young man he'd known and watched grow ever since he was four years old, as Carrie was now.

Clasping Sebastian's hand with both of his, he shook it warmly.

"Nice seeing you again, sir," Sebastian replied with equal feeling. "You're looking really well," he couldn't help adding. The man really did seem better now than before Sebastian had left Bedford.

James MacKenzie looked hardy and healthy and, except for the shafts of silver that were woven through his once dark, thick hair, he didn't look a day over fifty—even though Sebastian knew that he was.

"That's all Brianna's doing." Jim more than gladly gave his daughter the credit for saving his life, and for all but bringing him back from the dead. "She makes a great little dictator as well as an incredibly fine nurse," he said fondly. "And if it weren't for her, I don't mind telling you that I'd be pushing up daisies right this minute."

"Pushing them from where, Grandpa?" Carrie asked.

"We'll talk about that while Sebastian takes your mama out for a nice dinner," he promised. Not possessing a subtle bone in his body, Jim all but shooed the couple out the door. "You two better be going," he prodded, "if you want to get a good table. They go fast this time of the evening. And you *don't* want them putting you by the kitchen."

"We're going, Dad, we're going," Brianna assured him, knowing her father was afraid that she would find a reason at the last minute not to go.

As much as she wanted to come up with an excuse to bow out of the evening, she had a feeling that it would just be postponing things. This way, she'd endure the evening and then it would all be behind her.

After that, she thought, Sebastian would be on his way back to Japan or wherever and she could go back to living a quiet, normal life—such as it was.

"Don't hurry back," her father called after them as

they left the house. "I've got everything under control here."

I only wish I did, Brianna couldn't help thinking as she turned to wave goodbye to her daughter.

Chapter Six

Holding the car door open for her, Sebastian automatically looked down at Brianna's left hand as she slid into the passenger seat and then drew in her legs. He paused before closing the door.

Confusion mingled with a touch of relief when he saw that her ring finger was conspicuously unadorned. He wasn't sure exactly what made him look at her other hand, but when he did, he saw a small, tidy-looking diamond ring on the third finger.

Well, that answered *that* question, he told himself. Or so he believed.

"Change your mind?" he heard Brianna asking.

Caught between two streams of thought, Sebastian looked at her quizzically. He wasn't sure what she was referring to.

It hadn't gotten any clearer by the time he came around to the driver's side and got in. He glanced at her before buckling up.

"What?"

How did she tactfully word this without making it seem as if she was criticizing him? She gave it her best shot.

"Well, you were just standing there.... I thought that maybe you'd changed your mind about our going out for dinner."

Belatedly, he realized that he'd just frozen for a moment while she'd not only gotten into the car, but while she'd fastened her seat belt as well. He'd managed to close her door after a beat and had rounded the car to his side like a man trapped in a dream.

She'd probably thought he had turned into a village idiot, Sebastian upbraided himself.

"No, sorry, I guess I just got caught up in a thought."

He'd been staring at her and something was obviously either bothering him or distracting him. Either way, she wanted to know what this was all about. Otherwise, the awkward moments would only continue to pile up on one another.

"Something you'd like to share with the class?" she prodded, tongue in cheek.

For a second, he thought of just shrugging it off. The idea of saying something inane about needing to call his immediate superior in Japan crossed his mind as well. But any hastily constructed excuse would only be entrenching himself in a lie, and lies had a way of coming back and either biting you or blowing up on you when you least expected it. If nothing else, lies were hell to keep track of and usually became far too complicated to remember.

He had no desire to be caught in a lie. It was a long way back from that sort of thing.

"I was just looking at your ring," he told her, nodding at her right hand as he reached behind himself for the seat belt and buckled up.

At the mention of the ring, Brianna glanced down at her right hand. The engagement ring that J.T. had slipped onto her hand when he'd proposed to her had held such promise for her once. Now what it held was the memory of the man and what had almost been.

It also served to remind her that, for whatever reason, she just couldn't seem to get to the "finish line," couldn't even get to first base in that mystical land of "happily ever after."

Get a grip. He wants to catch up, not watch you sob into your salad.

Since Sebastian wasn't following up his statement with either a question or an observation, she felt obligated to say something herself and push the stillborn conversation along a little further.

"Carrie's father gave me this ring."

"Were you married long?" he asked Brianna out of the blue.

The question took her aback for a moment and she said the first thing that popped into her head. "No."

Which had to mean that her ex was a piece of work,

Sebastian concluded, because he knew Brianna. She wouldn't have just shrugged her shoulders and walked away from her marriage at the first sign of trouble. She was and always had been a fighter. He would bet his soul that she had tried to resolve whatever it was that had ended the union.

"I hope the divorce wasn't a drawn-out, nasty affair," he said with sympathy. "Those can really be hard on a kid, although your daughter does seem as if she's a very bright, well-adjusted little girl."

He was babbling now, Sebastian realized, and couldn't find the right place to stop without just abruptly shutting his mouth. He chastised himself for ever beginning the awkward topic.

"Sorry," he murmured. "Forget I said anything. It's none of my business."

The light ahead turned red and he brought his vehicle to a stop. That was when he became aware that Brianna had raised her hand and was waving it like a student.

"Yes, the girl in the front row," he responded, calling on her the way he would if this had actually been a classroom scene.

"I thought I'd rescue you before you wound up going too far in the wrong direction," Brianna told him.

Rather than clear anything up, she'd just confused the issue even further for him. "Too far in the wrong direction?" he echoed. It made even less sense to him when *he* said it than when she had. "What wrong direction am I taking it in?"

"There was no divorce—"

"You're still married?" he asked, stunned.

No, Brianna wasn't the type to step out on a husband, he told himself. And yet, how else was he to interpret her words? Was there a second husband? Taking what she'd said into account, did that mean that Carrie's father was an ex-husband whom Brianna had left behind? Some man she'd found too difficult to put up with and had gone on to shed before marrying someone else?

Or…?

"Light's green," she prodded just before the driver behind them lightly beeped his horn.

Sebastian quickly took his foot off the brake and put it back on the accelerator. As they drove down the next street, Brianna bit back a sigh.

"If you want the full, accurate story, you're going to have to let me talk in something a little bit longer than just sound bites," she told him.

He opened his mouth to protest, then realized that she was right. He *had* cut her off more than once. "Sorry. I guess I am jumping to conclusions," he allowed.

"More like you're pole-vaulting to them," she corrected. She searched for the most concise way to summarize the past few years. "Okay, to give you just the brief headlines—one, I'm not married—"

"Currently," he tacked on as if the word was the bow on the present.

"Okay," she allowed, letting him have his way for a second if it made him happy. "Currently. Two," she continued, her next words completely surprising him,

"I was *never* married. Consequently, three—since there was no marriage, there was no divorce."

He was still, he realized, utterly unenlightened about the state of her life. "Then are you still seeing Carrie's father?" he asked, becoming acutely aware of the fact that the thought of Bree being with another man, of seeing that man and creating a child with him, disturbed him far more than he'd thought possible. He knew, logically, that he had no right to feel that way.

She laughed softly to herself, despite the absence of humor in the situation.

"No," she answered, "I'm not seeing him. Not unless I'm doing a great deal of drinking. And just in case you're wondering, I don't drink more than a glass of wine at any given occasion."

Sebastian frowned in utter frustration. "I don't follow you."

"I'm not still seeing Carrie's father because he died in a boating accident a week before we were supposed to get married. I guess I'm just one of those people who's not meant to walk down the aisle."

There was a touch of ironic resignation in her voice. She'd grown up just assuming that a husband, marriage and children were in her future. Who knew she'd been assuming incorrectly?

He was putting together the pieces as fast as he could, but there were still edges that didn't fit. He had more questions. "And you had the baby after he died?"

"What baby?" she asked.

Were there more children? Children she hadn't introduced him to? Just how much *had* she changed in the past ten years?

"Carrie," he prompted.

He still hadn't gotten it straight, she realized. "I think that in order to get the right picture, you're going to have to do some more listening, Sebastian. *Silent* listening," she emphasized.

He turned right at the end of the block. "Okay," he agreed.

All right, from the beginning. "To start with, J.T. was Dad's partner at the hardware store. After Dad's near-fatal accident—" she still felt a cold shiver down her spine every time she thought of that "—J.T. ran the store all by himself, putting in eighteen-hour days. Dad would have lost the store if it wasn't for J.T." There was no mistaking the gratitude in her voice.

Was that why she'd gotten engaged to the man? Out of a sense of gratitude? Sebastian caught himself wondering. He realized that gratitude worked far better for him than thinking she'd done it out of love.

"Once I finally got Dad to the point that he decided he *was* going to recover, I took a second look at the store and knew I needed to pitch in.

"I guess J.T. and I grew closer. Couldn't pinpoint when or how, but we just did. He was a shoulder I could cry on, someone who would let me vent when I had to, and he never asked for anything in return." As far as she could see, the man was totally selfless. "But I sensed that he cared about me. A great deal. And then he had to deal with his own tragedy. He lost his wife in childbirth. I guess I helped him through that. He'd bring Carrie to work with him and we'd take turns taking care of her while one of us ran the store."

When she paused, he saw his opening. Sebastian couldn't help himself—he had to ask. "So then, is Carrie yours?"

"Yes."

There wasn't even a micromoment's hesitation on her part—because the child *was* hers. Carrie was locked away in her heart, and though she and the little girl didn't share a drop of the same DNA, they shared love and there wasn't anything she wouldn't do for Carrie.

"But not in the sense you mean," she added. "Carrie's mother died giving birth to her. She was an infant when J.T. and I became engaged. At four, I'm the only mother she's ever known, although I did tell her about her birth mother. She knows I adopted her."

He couldn't imagine how to start a conversation like that with a child. "Isn't four a little young for that?"

"Possibly," she allowed. "I do know that four is too young to be lied to," she told him. "I thought that if Carrie knew about her birth mother from the very start, she'd just accept things the way they are and not be bothered by the fact that she was adopted."

Brianna knew that she didn't owe him any kind of explanation, but she could sense that unanswered questions crowded his thoughts, so she proceeded to give him as much information as she thought was needed.

"When J.T. was killed, there was no next of kin to step up and adopt Carrie. She would have just been absorbed into the system, and I knew that J.T. wouldn't have wanted that. Hell, *I* didn't want that. J.T. did so much for my dad, I felt that adopting Carrie was the least I could do for him.

"So I petitioned to be allowed to adopt her. I held my breath for a whole year," she readily admitted, "putting up with unannounced spot checks where social workers would swoop down on their brooms, night or day, and just commandeer the premises. I had to stand back, let them go over everything with a fine-tooth comb and hope that I met whatever lofty requirements were in place at that particular time. I have no idea what they were expecting to find. Maybe they thought I was running a brothel," she speculated with a dry laugh.

"But in the end, you passed their inspections." It wasn't a guess on his part. No matter what else might have changed, he knew that much about Brianna. If she set her sights on something, she never backed off until she reached her goal.

Bree was stubborn that way.

She smiled now and nodded. "I passed their inspections," she confirmed. "And before you think I'm just being noble, I'm not. I love that little girl as if she was my very own and I couldn't begin to picture my life without her. Right now, if some long-lost relative came creeping out of the woodwork and claimed her, I don't know what I'd do," she confessed.

"Other than tie them up and dump them in the river?" he guessed.

"There is that," she acknowledged, managing to keep the grin off for a full fifteen seconds.

And then Sebastian nodded, thinking about what she had just told him. "It must have been very hard on you," he speculated, adding, "when Carrie's father was killed," in case he hadn't been clear in his comment.

Sebastian frowned. He hadn't used her late fiancé's name. He had no idea why he couldn't get himself to say the man's name, but he couldn't.

He was being petty and he knew it. After all, technically Sebastian had given up all claims to Bree when he'd walked out of her life. But though she had physically been out of his life for years now, she hadn't been entirely out of his thoughts.

Never, really.

She lingered in his mind like a song whose melody refused to fade away, as if threaded onto an endless loop.

"It was," she admitted with no fanfare, no dramatic pause. "I began to think that maybe I was jinxed." She looked at him. Did he think about her? After he'd gone off to college, had he spared her the occasional thought, or was she, then and now, being delusional? "Except that you at least didn't die. You just went away."

Sebastian searched for the slightest sound of blame or recrimination, for the accusation that he had just walked out on her when he should have remained at her side, offering his support and help.

But there wasn't any to be found.

Then again, Bree had never been one to throw blame

on anyone, even if they deserved it. She'd always just tried to carry the load on her own, always being the very personification of independence.

"About that," he began, picking his way through the possible minefield spread out ahead of him. "I should have stayed," he began. "After your dad's accident, I should have stayed with you." She'd been, he knew, all alone at the time.

"You should have done exactly what you did," she countered.

He looked at her, surprised.

But to her way of thinking, there was nothing to be gained from blaming him all these years later. It wouldn't get back even a minute of lost time and it certainly wouldn't make her feel vindicated.

"You were supposed to go on to get your degree and do what you love doing—teaching," she insisted.

"That wasn't the only place to get a teaching degree," he pointed out. He could have gone to a local college. Granted, it wouldn't have been as prestigious as the school he'd ultimately attended, but in the end, the knowledge he'd accumulated would have been the same. He was too determined to succeed.

But again, there was no need to rub any of that in.

It seemed to her that they had somehow switched sides on the argument, that he was picking up the banner that by all rights should have been hers and that she was backing what clearly sounded like his side of the argument.

"You're right—it wasn't. But the path you took led

you to your current job, and from what I can gather, that job makes you happy. In the final analysis, that means a great deal," she assured him. Shifting in her seat, she gazed out the window. She'd only been paying moderate attention to the route, but it was looking exceedingly familiar. "Where are we going?"

"I thought maybe we'd stop at Nate's," he said, mentioning the restaurant where they had sat for hours, scribbling their future on napkins and dreaming of the day they could finally get married. "I was surprised to find that the restaurant was still there," he confessed.

Brianna inclined her head. "Not all that much changes in Bedford," she reminded him.

Even as she said it, she couldn't help wondering if going to Nate's was really such a good idea. She hadn't been there since he'd left for college.

There was a reason for that. The place was fraught with memories.

Too many memories.

She had a feeling they would hit her the moment they walked into the place.

Can't be any more difficult facing the restaurant than it was facing Sebastian, Bree. You can do this— you know that.

She gave the mental pep talk her all, but nonetheless she still felt the tsunami gathering again in her stomach as Sebastian brought his car to a stop in the restaurant's parking lot.

Chapter Seven

It hit her the moment she walked in.

The ghosts of memories gone by. Dreams that never had a chance to take hold.

For just a second, Brianna felt herself catapulted back over the sea of years to another, far more innocent time. A time when she had been filled with such great hopes.

As she walked into the dimly lit atmosphere, she could feel anticipation pulsing through her, just as she had all those years ago.

Except that she wasn't that girl anymore. Now she knew better.

"Two?" the brightly dressed hostess in the soft peasant blouse and flowered skirt asked, looking from Sebastian to her.

"Two," Sebastian confirmed.

Why did that sound so lonely to her? Brianna wondered. It was like a promise that had lost its bloom and had been left to die, unfulfilled. "Two" used to sound so intimate, so powerful, like "two against the world."

But again, now she knew better.

"This way, please." Turning on her short, stacked heels, the hostess led the way through an already semifull dining area.

The restaurant hadn't changed at all, Brianna thought, quickly taking in her surroundings as she walked behind the hostess and just a step in front of Sebastian. Not one little bit. It looked just as if she had walked out of here only yesterday, instead of more than ten years ago.

There were the same eighteenth-century Early American decorations along the wall, including a blunderbuss she'd once admired. Back then, it had appeared real to her. Now she thought of it as all part of the make-believe world she knew that she'd inhabited back then.

"Is this all right?" the hostess asked politely, gesturing to a booth for two located just a shade away from the heart of the dining area.

The booth seemed almost too intimate, despite the fact that there were other tables, filled with patrons, all around that section of the room.

Brianna became aware that Sebastian was watching her. It was obvious that he was leaving up to her the final yea or nay on the seating arrangement.

She would have preferred being out in the middle of the room, but she heard herself saying, "It's fine," even though it really wasn't.

The booth, although not the one that they had usually occupied, was close enough in appearance and location to have passed for it, even upon close scrutiny.

After sliding in, Brianna accepted the menu that the hostess handed her.

Even with a table between them, she was acutely aware of Sebastian's nearness as he took the seat opposite her. The table might as well not have been there, for all the difference it made.

This felt even more intimate to her than when she'd danced with him last night. Why? After all, there was at least some space between them here, while there really hadn't been any last night.

Maybe her resistance against him was weakening, Brianna thought, concerned. Again she told herself that she shouldn't have gone to the reunion, shouldn't have agreed to have dinner with him like this tonight. She'd survived last night and she should have congratulated herself for that and tucked the whole thing away into some faraway box within her mind.

Sebastian studied her face and could almost read the tiny, telltale signs her thoughts left behind in their wake as they crossed her mind. Some things never changed.

"Something wrong?" he asked once the hostess had given him his menu and then retreated into the noisy dining area.

Startled, Brianna looked up. "No, nothing's wrong. Why?" she asked just a little too quickly.

"I don't remember you ever being this quiet," Sebastian told her.

Brianna shrugged, doing her best to look somewhat bored and disinterested. "Just sorting a few things out in my head," she replied rather vaguely.

His eyes never left her face. "Yeah," he said softly, "me, too."

She looked at him sharply when he said that. To her dismay, their eyes met and held for what felt like an endless, unsettling moment. She was tempted to ask just what it was that he was sorting out, but that would have left her open to the same question and, for the life of her, she had no acceptable answer.

The truth was she was just trying to deal with the ghost of a romance that was no longer even on life support. But there was no way she wanted to admit that to him right now.

Or *ever*.

Brianna looked so uncomfortable, he couldn't help noticing. Was that his doing? God, he hoped not. He could remember a time when there was nothing in the world more comfortable for either of them than sharing a conversation, or sharing a dream—or even just sharing the silence.

Back then it was as if Brianna was truly the other half of him. The part, he now realized, that made him better. A better man, a better person.

A better everything.

Sebastian searched for an opening. For something to say that would eventually lead him back to that place that he'd taken for granted because it had seemed so commonplace to him.

Back then he didn't have a real appreciation of just how special that niche actually was.

Sebastian suppressed a sigh. He supposed it went along with that old adage about never knowing what you had until you didn't have it anymore.

And now it was too late. Too late to reclaim anything. Too late to go back and start again.

"So, you became a nurse." He knew the words had to sound incredibly stilted to her, but he pushed on, hoping to somehow work out the kinks, to smooth out the dialogue so that it became more natural sounding.

He wanted, he silently admitted, to get back what they had lost.

What *he* had lost.

If only for a few hours.

"Yes, I did." She was almost certain that she had told him she was a nurse while they were dancing last night.

Dear God, had they run out of conversation already? she thought sadly. There'd been a time when they could literally talk for hours and never come close to running out of words.

But all that was in the past.

Before he had left her to deal with things on her own.

"Do you like it?" he asked. "Being a nurse," he added in case she'd lost the thread of the nearly stillborn conversation.

"Yes," she admitted with a smile, then said for good measure in case he thought she was just paying lip service to the sentiment, "Yes, I do."

"Why?" he prodded, curious about how she felt about

the career that seemingly had found *her* instead of the other way around.

The simple question took her aback and made Brianna think for a second. Back when they'd been together, she'd never had to explain anything to him. More often than not, Sebastian could literally intuit the way she felt about things.

But back then, they could end almost all of each other's sentences.

God, had she ever really been that young and innocent?

"Why?" she repeated, almost in disbelief that he should have to ask the question. "Because I like helping people. I like knowing that because of me, someone feels better, either in general or even just about themselves. That because of me, they've become more determined, or more hopeful." She smiled, more to herself than at him. "I guess working with my dad, bullying him into fighting his way back from despair and getting to a place where he could walk again and do what he did before the accident, showed me what a difference one person can make in another person's life.

"That was," she freely admitted to him, "enough to get me hooked. I really want to make that kind of a difference in other people's lives."

She stopped talking as her words echoed back to her. Brianna flushed ruefully. "I guess I must sound pretty full of myself to you."

After all, they no longer had that connection, that one-on-one way of communicating where each knew what the other was thinking. This man across from her was now a stranger.

"No," he contradicted her, "you sound like just what I need."

Only rigid control kept her mouth from dropping open. "Excuse me?"

He realized what that had to sound like to her. He didn't want her thinking he was trying to pick up where they'd left off years ago—even though he had to admit, if only to himself, that part of him was trying to do just that.

"I mean just what my mother needs," he amended, his eyes on hers to make sure she understood.

"Your mother?" She didn't understand. "Exactly why does your mother need me?"

His mother was a warm, outgoing person, but she was also a private person and he was fairly certain that she didn't want him broadcasting her recent change in condition. But this wasn't exactly the same thing. After all, Brianna was a medical professional as well as a woman of integrity. He knew she could be counted on to be discreet.

And he needed help.

"Well, I told you that my mother had a stroke recently...." His voice trailed off.

When he'd mentioned it last night, she'd just assumed from the way he talked that everything was under control. And since the severity of strokes had such a broad range, from the almost unnoticed to the debilitating, she had thought that his mother had been lucky.

Maybe not.

Brianna was aware of what havoc a bad stroke could cause, how one could ravage a person, reduce her to a shell of her former self. Was that the case, then? Had he just not wanted to talk about it until they were somewhere more private than a high school reunion?

"How bad was it?" she asked in a hushed voice. "Was her vision affected?"

He shook his head. "No, not that she mentioned."

"Thank God for that." And then she thought of another common symptom. "How about her speech? Does she have difficulty speaking?"

He thought for a moment, carefully reviewing their conversations, both over the phone and when he'd arrived. "No, that seems to be fine, actually. She's not slurring her words or anything close to that," he added with relief.

Okay, so far, so good, she thought. "Was there any paralysis? Face, arms, legs?" She recited each part as it occurred to her.

In response to each, Sebastian shook his head. As the gravity of the possible outcomes of his mother's stroke hit him, he realized just how large a bullet his mother had actually dodged. The wave of relief that came over him was enormous.

"I guess my mother was really pretty lucky," he concluded.

"Yes," Brianna agreed with feeling. "Yes, she certainly was." But now that the conversation had taken this route, she still had more questions. "What does the doctor say?"

He thought back to what his mother had said when he'd asked her the same thing. "That she'd had a stroke."

They obviously both already knew that. Brianna was looking for more than just that one terrifying piece of information.

"But you have talked to him, right?" she prodded. Brianna left the question up in the air, as if she took an affirmative answer for granted.

Frustrated, Sebastian was forced to shake his head again. "She doesn't want me fussing over her, or having to bother talking with doctors on what is supposedly my vacation. She told me that having me here for a visit was the best medicine in the world for her." A self-deprecating laugh left his lips. "I really wish I could stay indefinitely—"

She already knew where that sentence was going. "But your job isn't here," she concluded for him, doing her best not to sound dismissive. After all, this wasn't what he'd chosen to do with his life.

The moment she said that, their eyes met and she could see by the look on his face that he remembered when that sort of thing—finishing each other's sentences—happened on a regular basis.

But that was then and this was now, she reminded herself, struggling to maintain strict control over her emotions, because *now* had a completely different set of parameters.

"I'm not a doctor," she prefaced, verbalizing the disclaimer mechanically, "but I could take a look at her for you, talk to her and maybe assess the situation a little further for you if you'd like."

The broad smile on his lips gave her his answer before he even opened his mouth.

"That would be great," he told her. It was the first step in getting someone—preferably her—to stay on as his mother's companion/caretaker. But for now he wasn't going to push her. Instead, he said, "It would go a long way to putting my mind at ease about her condition, as well as helping me make decisions about what to do next."

She didn't want to ask what that meant, afraid that would make her think less of him. These days, so many people treated their parents like toys that had lost their usefulness, their appeal. After years of useful service, they were put out to pasture, so to speak.

"Like I said, I'm not a doctor," Brianna reminded him.

"No, you're not," he agreed. "But you worked a miracle with your father, using nothing more than your sheer determination—"

They'd both gotten lucky there, she couldn't help thinking—she and her father. She knew that he wouldn't have been able to accept facing life from the inside of a wheelchair. He *had* to walk again. There'd been no other alternative.

"But you just said that none of her limbs were affected by the stroke," Brianna pointed out. What kind of a miracle did he need for his mother? Had he omitted telling her something? Or were things worse than he'd initially let on?

"They're not," he agreed. "But anyone who can work the kind of miracle that you did on your dad is the kind of person I'd be more than happy about having around my mother. And don't forget that my mother already likes you."

This was going a little too fast for her liking. Somewhere along the line, she'd lost control of the situation.

"Wait, are we talking about just a plain visit, or is there something more extensive on the table that you forgot to mention?"

He looked at her with the soul of innocence, and she almost laughed out loud at his expression.

"Nothing on the table but just some French bread right now," he told her.

It just so happened that she made her living as a private-duty nurse rather than one who worked long shifts at the hospital, or in a doctor's office. And, as a private-duty nurse, she was on call over the course of the entire day. That was one of the reasons why she generally moved into the home of the person she was taking care of at the time. That way, she was assured of having Carrie with her in the evening.

Her father usually took care of the little girl during the daytime and then he'd drop his granddaughter off where she was staying after six. For now that worked out well for both Carrie and her. When it ceased to work, she would rethink her choice of nursing venue.

But Sebastian didn't know any of this. At least, she

hadn't told him that she was a private-duty nurse. At the moment she just assumed that Sebastian was asking her opinion on things, and that included whether to make use of a private-duty nurse.

Their waitress approached discreetly, waiting for a lull in the conversation. It occurred the moment Sebastian became aware of her presence. Since the menu hadn't really changed in all these years, making up their minds took almost no time at all.

Once the waitress left to give the chef their orders, Brianna asked, "When would you like me to come over to see your mother?"

He refrained from eagerly saying, "Now," and instead diplomatically inquired, "When would you be available?"

As it happened, her last assignment had just ended several days ago. Rather than accept the next assignment that the nursing agency offered, she'd opted to take a little time off. She wanted to spend some quality time with her family, especially the girl who seemed to be harboring feelings of neglect despite the attention Brianna's father was lavishing on her.

In addition, she just needed to have her batteries recharged. She'd been pushing too hard these past few months, doing too much, and it was draining her.

Seeing Sebastian had sufficiently recharged them—and then some.

In all honesty, it was now three days into the self-imposed "vacation" and Brianna was pretty much ready to get back to work. She'd never been one who was able to kick back for long stretches without feeling as if she was in the throes of nursing withdrawals.

Caring for children was an entirely different story, however. In general, she was accustomed to doing at least two, if not three, different things at once.

Even doing just one thing felt as if she was slacking off.

"I could clear some time tomorrow if you'd like," she offered.

"I wouldn't be taking you away from your work?"

"I consider it all part of the job," she told him, "and this would actually be mixing business with pleasure."

Then, in case he thought she was trying to revisit something they'd had in the past, she quickly told him, "I'd love to see your mother again."

"She still talks about you," he told her, leaving off the part about the fact that his mother viewed her as the one he allowed to get away.

"We kind of lost touch when…when my father was hurt," Brianna finally concluded, substituting that for the real reason she and his mother were no longer in communication. They'd lost touch because Brianna had been the one to break contact. Being around his mother had reminded her too much of him, of what she no longer had. Because, even then, she'd known in her heart that he wasn't coming back to Bedford after graduation.

And that had meant that he wasn't coming back to her.

The few conversations she and Sebastian had had after he'd left for college had been short, painful and exceedingly awkward, with far more left unsaid than was said.

And, just like that, the love of her life had become a stranger she had nothing in common with. Maybe they'd never meshed to begin with.

But sitting here opposite him now, she knew that all those things she'd told herself in those long, empty months after they had parted were just so many poor excuses. She *hadn't* stopped caring about him. There were still feelings, still longings pulsating between them. And most likely there always would be, until she was laid to rest six feet under.

And maybe even longer than that.

Chapter Eight

When he looked back on it later, Sebastian felt as if the majority of the evening had been spent in a singular space in time, divorced from any recriminations from past behavior.

Oh, once or twice—possibly even more—he'd caught himself wondering, "What if...?"

What if he hadn't left?

What if her father hadn't been in that accident?

What if she'd come with him and gone to the same college? They'd made plans to move in together and their goal from there had been marriage....

But wondering didn't make it so and didn't answer any of those questions.

At the end of the evening, as he walked Brianna to her door—the way he had walked her so many times in the distant past—he could have sworn they were moving in slow motion. Heaven knew it certainly felt that way to him, felt as if each moment was drawn out, stretched to the absolute limit.

Which might have explained why it seemed to take forever to reach her doorstep.

Yet, conversely, they found themselves there all too soon. Suddenly, there he was, looking down into her face, battling a myriad of emotions, all of which had popped up, dust and all, right out of the past. A past they'd once shared in the belief that it was just the first step toward an incredible future.

And one desire dominated it all.

He wanted to kiss her.

Wanted it so badly that he could all but taste it on his lips.

He knew he could murmur something like "For old times' sake" before he kissed her, but she wasn't a fool. She'd see through that in a heartbeat and more than likely ask him why he felt it was necessary to make an excuse for doing something that had once come so naturally to them.

"I had a very nice time tonight," Brianna said as she turned to face him on her doorstep. "To be honest, I really didn't think I would," she confessed. Not that it had exactly been a walk in the park. There'd been a third companion at the table with them. The ghost of summers past, when things had been so close to perfect and she'd thought that it would always be that way.

"Yeah, me, too," Sebastian responded. Was it his

imagination, or was she even lovelier in moonlight? All he knew was that there was a strong, all but overpowering ache in his gut right now.

"Which part are you agreeing with?" she asked, curious. "That you didn't think you were going to have a nice time, or that you actually *did* had a nice time?"

"Both," he answered.

The temptation to kiss her continued growing and getting stronger. So strong that, without thinking, he reached out to touch her hair, tucking a reddish strand behind her ear just the way he used to.

The tips of his fingers glided ever so lightly along her cheek, sending electric currents zapping along her sensitive skin.

She drew in her breath as her pulse began to beat faster.

Run! her brain pleaded.

If she let him kiss her, Brianna knew that any hope she had of keeping him at arm's length for his short visit would go up in flames.

With shaky knees, Brianna forced herself to turn away from him. She said something along the lines of "I'd better go in before my father sends out search parties to find me. I told him I'd only be gone a couple of hours."

And from where she was standing, it felt as if she'd been gone close to a decade.

Sebastian knew that if he pushed, even just the slightest bit, he could get her to stay out here with him a few moments longer. Knew, too, that if he lowered his mouth to hers, Brianna would be there to return his kiss.

But he also knew that it wasn't fair to either of them—especially to her—if he pressed his advantage. There was no point in starting something that had no hope of a future.

So, even though deep in his soul he didn't want to, Sebastian forced himself to step back. He inclined his head as he did so and said, somewhat amused, "Wouldn't want your dad grounding you on my account."

Was he laughing at her?

Brianna grasped at the feeling of indignation, knowing it was the only thing that might remotely save her from making a serious mistake and kissing *him* goodnight.

"I'm not 'afraid' my father's going to ground me—I'm just being thoughtful. I told him I'd be back by a certain time and I like keeping my word no matter what it's about."

Was that a dig? he wondered. A veiled reference to the fact that he'd once promised her that he would love her forever?

He couldn't fault her for thinking that he'd broken that promise—even though, now that he thought about it, he really hadn't. Because there was still a part of him that cared about her.

Cared a great deal.

So much so that the emotion in question might be

called *love* by those who were still innocent and believed in such things.

"Well, I still wouldn't want to be responsible for that," he told her, then paused before asking, "Are we still on for tomorrow?"

Dazed, relieved to have survived tonight, she looked at Sebastian and echoed quizzically, "Tomorrow?"

"You were going to come over to see my mother and tell me whether or not you thought she needed to have some extra care for a while." He'd ad-libbed the last part, doing his best to inch closer to the real reason he wanted her seeing his mother—to decide whether she could take her on as a patient.

"Oh, of course. Sure. I'll come by," she assured him quickly. "Is two o'clock all right?"

"Any time would be all right," he told her with sincerity. "I'll work my schedule around yours."

Well, *that* was certainly accommodating, she thought. Brianna flashed a neutral smile at him. "Then I'll see you tomorrow at two. At your mother's house. Same address?" she asked at the last moment, realizing that she was taking things for granted. After all, even though she hadn't moved, it didn't mean that other people hadn't.

Sebastian nodded. "Like you said, some things don't change. My mother's still living in the same house," he said. "She loves it far too much to ever consider moving. Believe me, I offered to help her downsize a few years ago by finding a condo for her, but she just wouldn't hear of it."

Brianna hardly heard what he was saying, her attention caught by something he'd said just before he'd told her that folksy story about trying to get his mother to move.

Was that what tonight was *really* all about? Had he set out to press a few of her buttons, make her recall all that they had once been to one another just so that she wouldn't turn him down when he asked her to see his mother?

Had he really turned that cool, that pragmatic? she silently questioned.

She didn't want the answer to be yes.

Maybe it would behoove her to think of Sebastian in that light. Because it just might help turn her into a pragmatist as well.

As she put her key into the lock and turned it, she knew that was not about to happen, not in this lifetime. She had no more of a chance of turning into a pragmatic, practical person than she did of becoming a firefly this fall.

Glancing at Sebastian over her shoulder, Brianna lingered just long enough to say, "Thanks again for dinner."

"No, thank *you* for agreeing to see my mother." He realized that as he said it, he was really already counting on her help, even though he knew he shouldn't. Brianna had every right in the world to give him a few words of assurance and then either move on, or, at most, give him a referral to another nurse.

Initially, after the all but paralyzing fear that his mother had suffered a debilitating stroke had faded, that was all that he'd wanted—to find a competent nurse to look after his mother until she was out of the danger zone.

But the moment he'd realized that Brianna had gone on to become a nurse, he knew that he wouldn't be satisfied with anyone else. Wouldn't be satisfied with anything less than having Brianna sign on as his mother's private-duty nurse for the duration.

He trusted her. Trusted her with his mother's welfare. With his mother's life.

Because he knew Brianna's ethics, knew how determined she could be. Knew that to place his mother's fate in her hands was really the very best thing he could do for his mother.

Don't push too hard, he warned himself now. *At least, not yet.*

He needed to completely win Brianna over first. Since she had always liked his mother, half the battle had already been fought and—as near as he could figure it—won.

"Tomorrow, then," he repeated, then quickly turned on his heel and walked back to his car. He was fearful that he might ruin everything, because just at the last moment, he'd had another quick, strong surge of desire to pull her into his arms and find out if her kiss still made him weak in the knees.

Brianna quickly slipped into her house, incredibly relieved.

And just as incredibly disappointed.

Back in Bedford just a few days, and already he was

making her crazy. Sincerely hoping to dodge her fate at the last moment, she was nonetheless doomed.

Putting on her best face as she braced herself for the onslaught of questions, she went to find her father and get it over with.

"Oh, my sweet Lord, you haven't changed one little bit!" Barbara Hunter cried the moment she saw the woman she'd once thought was going to be her daughter-in-law come walking into her living room.

Entrenched in her role of recovering stroke victim, Barbara was sitting propped up on the sofa, a blanket tucked around her lower half at Sebastian's insistence, and half a dozen small, colorful pillows tucked against her back, also at Sebastian's insistence.

He'd been so thoughtful and considerate from the second he'd rushed to her side that her conscience was making it difficult for her to all but breathe. She didn't like lying to him this way. The whole thing bothered her a great deal.

It would have been bothering her a great deal more if it wasn't for the fact that she knew in her heart of hearts that she was doing this for Sebastian's own good. That she was pulling out all the stops, using everything she had at her disposal, not just to bring together what she'd always considered the perfect couple, but to keep them together until they both realized how very right they were for each other.

And when Sebastian would eventually forgive her—

after the truth had, perforce, come to light—he would understand why she'd done what she had.

But all that was still to come. Right now she had Brianna before her—and a part to play. She had to be on her toes, because Brianna was sharp.

Brianna took the hands that were warmly extended to her, squeezing them affectionately, if ever so lightly. She looked at Sebastian's mother in complete wonder.

She had to admit that she was expecting to see a woman who looked a great deal more frail. For someone who had recently had a stroke, Barbara Hunter appeared amazingly well for her ordeal, almost like the picture of health.

But then, Brianna knew, appearances could be exceptionally deceiving—especially with artfully applied makeup.

Smiling at Barbara as she went to occupy a tiny corner of the sofa beside Sebastian's mother, she said, "I could say the same thing about you, Mrs. Hunter. Your color is amazingly good," she told the older woman in complete awe.

Barbara leaned forward just a tad and confided, "Makeup does wonders," as she dismissed the compliment.

Although she didn't make any sort of regular pilgrimages to the makeup counters in her local malls, Brianna could tell the difference between a face that was only made up to look good, or, as in this case, to look healthy, and a face that actually *was* healthy.

Scrutinizing her, she decided that Barbara Hunter definitely belonged in the second category.

Which, all things considered, seemed rather unusual to Brianna. Something was off.

But she hadn't come to argue—she had come to see if she could offer advice or even a little help. It completely delighted her that Sebastian's mother was not nearly as unwell as Sebastian had first led her to believe.

Was that because the woman had managed to bounce back, making an absolutely astounding recovery, or could he be using his mother to get her to come around, to forgive him and possibly even give them another chance...?

No, she told herself in the next nanosecond. That would mean that Sebastian had turned into a manipulative person, and she didn't want to believe that about him. Didn't want to think of him in that light.

Instead, Brianna preferred to think that his mother was one of the extremely lucky ones whose bodies had issued a warning to them and then just gone back to normal. Back to "business as usual."

"Sebastian told me you had a stroke last week," she said gently.

Was it her imagination, or did the woman's smile suddenly look a little strained?

And if so, why?

Because she didn't want to talk about her ordeal, or because there'd *been* no ordeal?

Brianna's intuition leaned a certain way. Because

this was Sebastian's mother, she decided to dismiss this thought.

"I did," Barbara answered, her voice rather low and somewhat shaky. Was that pain she detected in the older woman's voice?

Or uncertainty?

"I know it's an uncomfortable subject to talk about," Brianna said. "The very thought of it touches on our mortality, but anything you can tell me about the incident—" such a nice, clinical word, she thought, for something so ugly "—would be very helpful."

"Helpful?" the older woman questioned, her thin eyebrows drawing together like an animated line.

"Bree is considering whether or not to take your case, Mom," Sebastian said, interrupting.

Brianna didn't see the hopeful flash in his mother's eyes, but he did.

It made him wonder.

Was the flash there because it made her feel better, having someone she knew looking to help her? Or was there some other reason behind that look?

His life abroad had made him too suspicious, Sebastian thought self-critically. His mother wasn't some conniving schemer—she was a down-to-earth, simple woman who lived alone and who had been understandably frightened by her ordeal. Of course the thought of having someone she knew around to look after her pleased her.

He was searching for hidden meaning where there was none, he thought, chastising himself.

Sebastian rose to his feet. "Why don't I leave the two of you alone to talk?" he suggested, thinking that his presence might make it awkward for his mother to talk about what had happened to her.

"That might not be a bad idea," Brianna agreed.

"Thank you," his mother said to him, looking relieved.

"I'll be in the family room if you need me," he said. And with that, he left the room.

Chapter Nine

"So tell me, what's going on?" Brianna asked Barbara Hunter as soon as her son had left the room. She took a seat on the chair opposite the sofa and focused all her attention on the woman.

Barbara looked at her, doing her best to hide her nervousness. She'd never been good at lying and she knew it. At times, when the truth sounded as if it was a tad suspicious, she'd be nervous that what was coming out of her mouth *sounded* as if she was lying.

And now, given the fact that everything she'd told Sebastian in order to get him to come stateside in time for his high school reunion had been based on a ruse, Barbara felt as if she was knee-deep in falsehoods and bald-faced lies.

Did Brianna suspect?

Could the young nurse tell just by looking at her that she hadn't had a stroke?

By asking what was "going on," was Brianna asking about her symptoms, or the reason behind the fabrications and lies?

Barbara licked her lips to keep them from sticking together. They were bone dry. Even so, she stopped herself before she could moisten them, afraid that the simple act—and the reason for it—would give her away to someone as sharp-eyed as Brianna.

"I'm afraid I don't understand what you mean," Barbara managed to respond quietly, stopping just short of sucking in air as her lungs felt suddenly depleted of oxygen. Lying created the sensation of breathlessness within her.

Maybe she hadn't made herself clear, Brianna thought. His mother looked genuinely uncomfortable and confused. Was that because of the stroke? Or was there some other reason for the woman's discomfort? She certainly hoped that *she* wasn't the cause for the woman's reaction.

Sebastian's mother had always been nothing but warm and friendly toward her, making her feel welcome any time she came over to the house with Sebastian. Making her feel, back then, as if she was already part of the family.

Brianna remembered thinking when she first met his mother that she would have loved, if she were able to pick and choose, to have a mother just like Barbara Hunter.

The very last thing in the world she wanted was to make that woman feel uncomfortable in her presence.

"Are you feeling any physical discomfort right now?" Brianna rephrased. When the other woman shook her head in response, Brianna pressed on. She needed to get her own clear picture of events. "Just what exactly initially alerted you to the fact that you were having a stroke?"

Barbara released the breath that had gotten trapped in her lungs. She felt a little more at ease now. She'd done her homework on this one, looking up on the internet the condition she was feigning. She was rather proud of herself for that, seeing as how navigating on the computer was completely foreign to her.

Admittedly, it had been hard for her at first, but Maizie had shown her how to get around something she referred to as "a search engine," which wasn't an engine at all, just something that allowed her to type in a few key words, in exchange for which she was shown a plethora of things called "websites." And those in turn gave her the information she was looking for—eventually.

It had taken her a while, granted, but now she felt that she was adequately educated regarding the subject matter and ready for any questions that her son might have for her.

Or, in this case, that the young woman she'd hoped her son would someday marry might have for her.

Given the question, Barbara now recited the symptoms chapter and verse, which she'd previously memorized, citing things like "dizziness, nausea and a really rapid heartbeat."

"I thought my heart was going to fly right out of my chest," Barbara told her with just the right touch of earnestness.

"Did you lose consciousness?" Brianna asked.

Barbara paused, trying to remember the right response to that question. She wanted Brianna to think she'd had a mild stroke, one that hadn't resulted in any sort of permanent damage. Other than simplifying her story, it also made it easier for her to have fewer details to keep straight. She knew very well that she couldn't sustain a multilayered performance for an indefinite length of time.

"No," she finally answered with a note of triumph in her voice. "I didn't. I was conscious the entire time."

"Well, that's good," Brianna said with genuine satisfaction. "How did you get to the hospital?"

For a second, the relatively simple question threw her. But after a moment, drawing on her past experiences, Barbara had her alibi in place.

"My friend drove me to the hospital. I called Maizie and told her what I was feeling. She came over right away and whisked me off to the E.R."

Brianna nodded, pleased. She knew that the faster a patient with stroke symptoms received medical attention, the greater the possibility of reversing any damage. Those first crucial minutes made the difference between recovery and all sorts of debilitating effects, ending with paralysis.

That being the case, she needed to get more of a handle on all this. "Would you happen to know how much time passed from the first onset of your symptoms to your arriving at the E.R. and receiving treatment?"

She knew that one, Barbara thought with a tinge of frustration setting in. She really did. So why couldn't she think of it now?

Barbara hesitated for a moment, sifting through the various pieces of information she'd read and absorbed, trying to remember the right answer.

"About an hour altogether. Maybe a few minutes more than that," she added hesitantly. "Maizie's office is close by," she interjected, "and she came the second I called her."

"You're lucky to have a friend like that," she told the other woman.

"In more ways than one," Barbara murmured, then, realizing she'd said that out loud, she flashed a wide smile at the young woman.

Brianna wondered what she meant by that, but there were more important questions to ask Mrs. Hunter at the moment.

"And how are you feeling now?" Brianna asked.

"A lot better—but still rather weak," Barbara quickly added.

Heaven forbid that Brianna thought she didn't need any sort of home medical care. That was the whole point of this, to keep throwing Brianna and her son together until they came to their senses and the spark reignited between them.

The young woman, she recalled, was honest to a fault. That sort of person did not charge for services she felt weren't necessary.

Brianna leaned forward just a tad, her blue eyes peering into the other woman's soft brown ones. "You're not disoriented?" she asked.

Barbara was watching the young woman's face, trying to take her cue from her expression. She decided that she wouldn't want to play poker against Brianna, especially since the younger woman's expression was almost unreadable.

Barbara was left to her own devices as to how to answer, so she replied cautiously. "Maybe a little fuzzy around the edges at times."

"That's all perfectly natural," Brianna told her. "Tell me, were you ever diagnosed as having angina or A-fib?"

Barbara knew what the first condition was and shook her head. "No to angina," she said with confidence. But her confidence tapered off as she asked, "But what's A-fib?"

"Sorry, I shouldn't have just thrown letters at you. It stands for atrial fibrillation." The look on the older woman's face said she was no more enlightened, so she broke it down for Barbara into the simplest terms. "What it means is, have you experienced any rapid heartbeat or skipped beats?"

Until this moment, Barbara had just assumed that everyone had that happen to them on one occasion or another. She still felt relatively safe in her assumption, so she thought it would be all right to answer in the affirmative. "Yes. Sometimes," she qualified.

Brianna went to the next logical question, which in this case involved prescriptions. "Which beta-blocker did the doctor prescribe for you to treat that?"

Barbara's mind went to a terrifying blank. "I'm not sure," Barbara answered evasively.

"That's okay—lots of people forget the name of the pills they're required to take." She rose to her feet. "Where do you keep your medicine?" Brianna asked, perfectly content to do her own legwork. "I'll just take a quick peek at what's there and—"

Barbara panicked. There *was* no heart medication of any kind, because she'd made up the whole thing. She desperately needed a way to distract Brianna.

"Is it hot in here?" Barbara asked suddenly, futilely fanning herself with her hand. "Do you feel warm?" She swayed slightly as she tried to get up. "Oh, I feel so weak, so dizzy...."

Brianna was back beside her in a moment, her arms going around the other woman's girth. Despite its size, she felt she had a good grip on Sebastian's mother. Only then did she ease Barbara back onto the sofa.

"You've got to be careful about making any sudden moves," Brianna gently cautioned her. "Let me check your heart rate," she requested.

Her slender fingers already on the woman's wrist, she searched for Barbara's pulse. Placing two fingers over the quickly vibrating area, Brianna silently counted the rapid beats.

Brianna frowned slightly as she released the wrist. "Certainly feels like A-fib to me." She took note of Barbara's expression and misinterpreted its origin. "Don't look so worried, Mrs. Hunter. I'm sure your doctor told you that the condition is totally controllable. You'll be back running those literacy courses of yours at the library in no time," she promised.

As Brianna began to turn away, Barbara caught her hand. She dispensed just the right amount of truth to get what she wanted. "If it's all the same to you, dear, I'd like to take my time getting better." Her eyes met the young woman's. "I had a friend who rushed back into her day-to-day life right after she had a similar incident, and she wound up in the hospital with another stroke, far worse than what she'd had the first time around. I don't want the same thing happening to me."

Brianna gave her a reassuring smile. "I understand perfectly and I didn't mean to make you think anyone's rushing you to do something you don't feel ready for. Everyone has their own inner pace," she added. "And you have to be true to yours."

"This 'incident' has its upside," Barbara confided. "I mean, it did bring Sebastian rushing back to see me." Her mouth curved fondly as she spoke about her son. "He wasn't going to come for a visit until December, if then." When Brianna raised an eyebrow, she explained. "Things have a habit of coming up at the last minute in his world, and he's canceled trips to the States before," she said with a sigh.

"Oh."

A few things clicked into place in Brianna's head, but she didn't want to say anything out loud just yet. If she was wrong, she'd be guilty of offending Sebastian's mother and she didn't want to do that. She had a feeling, though, that for whatever reason, Barbara wasn't being entirely truthful about what had happened and her condition. Just how much was true and how much wasn't, she didn't know, but Brianna was certain of one thing.

"Sebastian would be relieved to know that you're not standing at death's door with a Now Serving number in your pocket," she pointed out diplomatically. The expression on Barbara's face did not match that of a woman whose mind had been set completely at ease. "What would you *like* me to tell him?" she asked, qualifying the word *like*.

"That I'd feel a great deal better and more confident if I had someone staying with me for a little while."

"You mean him?" Brianna assumed that getting Sebastian to stay for an extended period of time was the woman's ultimate goal.

"Like a nurse," Barbara corrected.

Brianna needed to be perfectly clear on this. She'd initially thought Sebastian was just asking for an evaluation of his mother's condition so he'd know what he needed to do for her.

"Mrs. Hunter, are you asking me to take you on as a patient?" Brianna asked.

Barbara looked at her hopefully, as if she were mentally crossing her fingers. "Could you?" she asked.

Well, her schedule *was* clear, but she needed to get

a few things out in the open and understood first. "I usually move in for the duration of a patient's care."

Barbara nodded. "Even better—I'd feel more secure knowing you were close by," she quickly added.

There was one more very important thing. "Mrs. Hunter—"

Barbara held up her hand, stopping her. "Barbara, please," she requested. "If you're going to be here taking care of me, you should at least be able to call me by my first name," she told the younger woman with a smile.

"I don't move in by myself," Brianna began.

Barbara nodded. "Oh, I'm sure that Sebastian wouldn't mind helping you bring your things over here," she assured Brianna.

Physical logistics was not the problem. She was strong enough to carry her own things. This was far more important than moving suitcases. This was, in essence, the deal breaker if she got the wrong answer.

"No, what I'm trying to tell you is that I'd be bringing my four-year-old daughter, Carrie, with me."

Sebastian had already told her about Brianna's daughter. He'd been so taken aback initially and then just blown away by the scope of the little girl's mind, he'd shared the whole story with her.

After her initial surprise—much like his, she suspected—she'd summoned her courage and gotten on the phone with Brianna's father, a man she'd met briefly at a couple of PTA meetings dating back to when their children were in their last year of high school. After identifying herself, she'd asked him to supply the rest of the answers she needed.

The man had been quite helpful once he understood what she was attempting to do. And he'd been exceedingly charming as well. She'd stayed on the phone quite a while.

"I would insist on it," Barbara told her now. "A child belongs with her mother. Especially a little girl." The soul of innocence, she went on to ask, "Is there anything else?"

"Yes," Brianna replied. "When would you like me to start?"

"The sooner the better," Barbara told her in all honesty. Taught to always seal the bargain, she put her hand out. "So it's a deal?"

Brianna slipped her hand into his mother's, feeling as if she was taking advantage of the other woman. She was sealing a bargain that seemed just far too advantageous for her.

But, for whatever reason, Barbara Hunter truly felt she needed to have her around and to make use of her services. The first rule about nursing was to make the patient feel better, so she was not about to argue the point with the woman.

"It's a deal," Brianna confirmed.

Barbara's grin widened even more.

Brianna stopped moving and just watched her father in uncertain awe.

"You know, if I didn't know any better, I'd say that

you were eager to get rid of me," she told him. For the first time in her recollection, her father was helping her pack her things as well as Carrie's beloved collection of toys and books. Clothes were only incidental to Carrie and not nearly as important as her possessions.

"Eager to get rid of you?" her father echoed, then declared, "Never," in a voice that could have easily belonged to the hero of a melodrama. "I'll be standing by the window, my face pressed against the glass, a candle burning in each hand the entire time that you're going to be gone."

Brianna laughed and resumed selecting and discarding various articles of clothing.

"Very funny. I guess, after all this time, you're probably looking forward to having the house all to yourself," she surmised.

"I promise to keep the wild parties down to a minimum," he quipped.

"How are you going to party?" she asked. "I thought you were going to be standing with your face pressed against the glass, holding a candle in each hand, remember?" she asked, doing her best to sound as if she was at least semiserious.

"Man's gotta eat and take a couple of bathroom breaks occasionally," her father pointed out. "That's why the parties'll be kept to a minimum."

She shook her head. Inside every man was still a wild, spirited teenager, she couldn't help thinking. "Well, you're certainly old enough not to need a lecture."

Her father laughed. "Knew getting old was good for something."

She paused to pat his cheek. "You're not old, Dad, just a little slightly used," she told him fondly.

Looking around the room, she and her father had managed to pack everything she and Carrie were going to need for what she hoped was a short duration. Otherwise, she was going to have to make a few trips back. She supposed that wasn't really a bad thing. It would allow her to look in on her father.

She turned toward him now. "You know where to find me if you need me."

She'd given him the phone number as well as the address the moment she'd walked in. "It's on the refrigerator. You wrote the number in letters big enough for a helicopter pilot to see if he was circling the house."

"If a helicopter pilot is circling the house, we'd have bigger problems than you seeing the phone number I wrote." She grew serious for a moment. He, along with her daughter, had always been her first priority. Time hadn't changed that. "You'll be okay?"

"I'll miss you," he told her. "And the pip-squeak," he added, referring to Carrie. "But I'll muddle through." He kissed the top of her head. "You just go do what you do best. Bully some patient into getting well," he instructed fondly.

"Between you and me," she confided, "I think she's halfway there already."

He looked at her for a moment, wondering just how

much his daughter suspected. Bree had always been a very sharp girl.

"Then this should be a piece of cake for you," he told her. "Speaking of which, I picked one up for you this afternoon when you called to say you were taking on a new case. It's waiting for you in the kitchen whenever you and the pip-squeak want a break."

"Cookies-and-cream?" she asked. It had been her favorite flavor since she was fourteen.

He grinned at her. "Would I get anything else?"

She brushed a quick kiss against his cheek. "You're one in a million, Dad."

"I know." He laughed, putting an arm around each of "his girls." "Let's go break the cake in."

Together, they went to the kitchen to do justice to the cake he'd bought.

Chapter Ten

He was pacing.

Sebastian forced himself to stop. The thing of it was, he hadn't been aware that he was doing it until just now.

This was stupid. Why was he pacing and looking out at the driveway every time he passed the window? He was an adult, not a kid fresh out of puberty. It wasn't supposed to matter to him one way or another if Brianna moved into his house.

His house.

He laughed shortly. After all this time, he still thought of the place where he'd grown up as *his* house. His home. His home even though for the past four years, he'd lived in a sleek, ultramodern apartment in Tokyo.

But *this* was home and Brianna was moving into it. And despite his attempt at a devil-may-care, nonchalant attitude, he kept right on glancing through the window. Moreover, he was listening for the sound of an approaching vehicle.

And when he finally heard it, his damn pulse quickened.

To make matters worse, when he turned, he nearly tripped over his mother's damn cat. Stopping short of just clipping the feline's nose with the tip of his shoe, he managed to catch himself just in time.

He bit back a curse. "Damn it, Marilyn, you're going to wind up flatter than a pancake if you don't stop getting in my way."

Marilyn strolled out of the way, completely unfazed by the fate she'd almost suffered.

When Brianna pulled up into the driveway—at exactly the time she'd told his mother she would arrive—he was at the front door before she had even turned off the CR-V's engine.

Getting out of the vehicle, she looked at Sebastian quizzically. Had there been a change in plans? She couldn't think of another reason for him to have come out to meet her car so quickly.

"Hi," she said a bit uncertainly, waiting for him to say something that would tell her what was going on.

But all Sebastian said in response to her greeting was a more formal "Hello."

Rounding the hood, she made her way over to the passenger side and then opened the rear door.

"We're here, honey," she told Carrie as she leaned in and began removing her daughter from her car seat.

Sparing Sebastian a glance, she gave in and finally asked, "What are you doing here?"

He'd been asking himself that all day. He said, "I used to live here, remember?"

"Yes, I know that. That's not what I meant." *And you know it.* "You came out the minute my tires hit your driveway. Something wrong?" she asked. She scooped Carrie up in her arms and then set her down.

Carrie's attention, like her own, was focused on Sebastian.

"No," he replied, wondering why she would think there was something wrong—other than his having stepped out of her life for the past ten years. "I just thought I'd see if you needed any help moving in."

Something told her that wasn't all, but she let it go. Maybe she was just overthinking things. She'd been doing that since she'd bumped into Sebastian—and all those memories—at the reunion.

"Oh, well, that's nice of you," Brianna acknowledged.

"Despite what you might think, I *can* be a nice guy."

It was on the tip of her tongue to say something that would put the veracity of his statement in doubt, but what was the point of that? Of rehashing everything? The past was gone and there was no going back and fixing it or changing it. She knew that.

So instead, she said, with a complete economy of emotion, "Never said anything else." Then, wanting to change the subject as quickly as possible, Brianna went on to tell him, "And just so you know, I'm not 'moving in.' I'm just in a temporary holding pattern until your mother feels more secure about managing her day-to-day life on her own."

He shifted so that he was directly in front of her just as she was about to open up the vehicle's hatchback door. "You really think she'll be able to?" Sebastian asked.

"No doubt in the world," Brianna answered him honestly. "From our little talk yesterday, I got the feeling that your mother is really a lot better than she thinks she is. She just needs to have her confidence restored and bolstered a little. Once that happens, Carrie and I will be on our way again, riding off into the sunset," she added wryly.

"Like the Lone Ranger," he quipped, amused at the image she used.

Both Brianna and Carrie chimed in together, "Who?"

"Obviously your education has a hole in it," he said, then decided to fill them in. "The Lone Ranger was a lone survivor of an outlaw raid on a company of Texas Rangers. He was nursed back to health by an Indian he'd befriended as a young boy. After he recovered, he put on a mask and rode around the countryside on a white stallion, fighting injustice wherever he found it. He always handed out a silver bullet before he rode away."

"Did he shoot the silver bullet?" Carrie asked.

She'd been so quiet that, for a moment, he'd completely forgotten she was there. "No, I think he just saved them to hand out as souvenirs. Presents," he amended, thinking she wouldn't understand what the other word meant.

Carrie gave him a look that was at once resigned and ever so slightly irritated. "I know what a souvenir is," she told him.

"Sorry." Despite his apology, Sebastian was unable to suppress a grin. The little girl just kept surprising him.

As far back as he could remember, it had been just his mother and him. His father was a soldier who'd perished halfway around the world. Sebastian had grown up always looking for ways to bring in a little money and help his mother. He'd gone through a nostalgic period early in his life, picking through garage sales and the like, looking for old movie and television memorabilia in the hope of stumbling across something rare that would bring in a sizable amount of money. He had wound up getting hooked on old movies and classic TV programs for a while, before deciding his time and effort could be better spent elsewhere.

But the Lone Ranger had always remained one of his favorites. He supposed that was because, at one point in his life, he had identified with the loner who, after having gone through typical—at least for those times—childhood and young adult years, had a life-altering experience that left him with only one friend he felt he could trust.

One friend was all that was necessary when it counted. And his "one friend" had been Brianna.

That, too, was in the past, he reminded himself.

About to comment on the little girl's rather extensive

vocabulary, the remark evaporated from his lips as he looked into the rear of Brianna's car.

From what he could see, it was completely filled.

He glanced back at Brianna, then looked again into the interior of the vehicle. For someone who'd claimed not to be moving in, she'd brought everything with her but the kitchen sink.

"Are all these suitcases filled with clothes?" he asked incredulously, gesturing at the squadron of dark gray cloth suitcases that were packed so tightly together, had they been people, they would have suffocated.

"No, actually they're filled with stuffed animals and books," she corrected. She could tell that he was looking at her to see if she was kidding. She wasn't. "There's just one suitcase with clothes," she told him. "Both of our clothes," she clarified, adding, "Carrie and I don't require much in the way of clothing. She just needs a few changes of play clothes, and I'm in a uniform most of the time."

"You don't have to be if you'd rather not," he told her.

Brianna's mind froze for a moment. Was he telling her she could dress casually, or was he telling her that she didn't need to dress at all?

You're getting too carried away. That's not what he's saying and you know it. For one thing, his mother's here. For another, he wouldn't take a chance on traumatizing Carrie.

Sebastian had always liked children and he could be counted on to be the first to take note if anything was being done to harm a child, even indirectly.

"What do you mean?" she asked.

He'd thought it was obvious, but explained anyway. "You can wear casual clothes if that makes you feel more comfortable. I think my mother wants you to feel right at home here."

"And I want her to feel as if she's being well taken care of and watched over. I think the uniform, however subliminally, might just reinforce that feeling for her. Besides, it's a nurse's uniform, not a suit of armor to be worn during a summer heat wave," she pointed out. "But, thanks," she tagged on, in case he thought she was just being argumentative and difficult. "I do appreciate knowing I have leeway."

Picking up the lightest container, she handed it to Carrie, then took another, far heavier one herself. "If you could point out which bedroom is going to be ours, that would be great."

He picked up two suitcases, one in each hand, then led the way up the driveway to the front door. "Follow me," he told her.

"We will," Carrie piped up with assurance, the voice of a seasoned adult trapped within the body of a small child.

Sebastian pressed his lips together to keep the laugh that rose in his throat right where it was. Turning, he pushed the unlocked front door open with his back and then went to the staircase.

"It's the second room to the right," he told his two-woman entourage.

The first room to the right at the top of the stairs was *his* bedroom, Brianna remembered.

Or at least it had been that one night when they'd discovered each other, and a whole new world had opened up for them.

Or for her, at any rate.

She did her best not to glance toward the room when she reached the landing, but a wave of nostalgia got the better of her. Her eyes darted toward it before she was able to rein herself in.

"Almost there, Carrie," she told her daughter.

It proved unnecessary because the high-pitched voice responded, "I can see that."

Unlike Sebastian, Brianna made no effort to hold back a laugh. "Yes, I'm sure you can. Find a place for that box and we'll go back down for more," she told the little girl. She foresaw *many* trips up and down the stairs today—and possibly an aching back by day's end.

Still holding the box she'd brought up the stairs, Carrie slowly looked around the room, as if seeking just the right spot to house her beloved treasures.

Brianna noticed the curious look on Sebastian's face and guessed at what was going on in his head.

"Location's everything," she explained to him. "Carrie is extremely organized for a four-year-old."

He knew CEOs who subscribed to more chaos than this child apparently did. "She's very organized for *any* age," he corrected.

His observation earned him a wide smile from Carrie that she flashed his way.

Finally making her decision, Carrie walked with determined steps to the area beside the window, then set her box down beneath it.

"It's nice over here. The sun makes it bright. They'll be happy here," she declared.

Brianna glanced toward Sebastian, anticipating his reaction. His eyebrow was raised in a silent query. He was probably asking her the identity of the "they" Carrie was referring to.

"Her stuffed animals," she told him. "She likes to make sure they're comfortable in their new surroundings. It reminds her to think of others before herself," she added.

Carrie was already by the bedroom door. "Can I go down and get some of the others, Mama?"

"Not without me," she reminded Carrie. "You know that."

"I don't want them to get too hot in the car," she explained, trying to give her mother a reason for her sudden break in protocol.

"I think the extra minute or two won't make a difference to them," Brianna assured her daughter.

But even so, she was already leading the way back downstairs. Carrie matched her, step for step, all but leaping to make up for the difference in stride.

Watching the interaction with no small amount of awe, Sebastian brought up the rear.

"Give me the heaviest one," he told Brianna when they'd returned to her car again.

"The heaviest one, huh?" Was he being gallant, or

just macho? Either way, she needed the box out of the car. "That would be the big box in the rear," she told him. "It's packed with her books."

It had taken both her father and her to lift the container and put it into the car. Leaning in now, she pulled the edge of the box over to her a little at a time until she was *finally* able to get it to the edge of the vehicle.

"And it's pretty heavy. Since we're going to be staying on the second floor, maybe we should just unpack the box and bring the books up an armload at a time," she suggested.

"Or I could just take it upstairs for you and save a lot of time," he told her, hefting the large box out of the car.

"It's too heavy," she insisted.

Her words fell on deaf ears.

She should have expected nothing less, she thought. Sebastian could be very stubborn when he wanted to be. Before babies, reality and responsibilities, she could afford the luxury of being reckless and throwing caution to the winds. But no more.

"Careful," she warned, moving out of his way. "Or I'll wind up having to nurse you through the aftermath of a hernia operation."

"If that's supposed to get me to put down the box, it's not working," he told her. "You're going to have to come up with something better than that," he said as he passed her and crossed the threshold leading into his house.

Bracing the contents in his arms as best he could, he made his way up the stairs, moving a tad more slowly than he would have liked. He didn't want the cardboard suddenly to give way and an avalanche of books to come pouring out.

"I forgot how stubborn you could be," she said in a rare display of exasperation.

"Funny, I was going to say the same thing about you," Sebastian answered.

"Mama says it's not nice to be stubborn," Carrie told him, putting her small body in his direction.

"Except at certain times," Brianna felt she had to qualify.

"Is this one of those times?" Carrie asked, turning her face up to her mother.

"I'm afraid it certainly looks that way," she told the little girl, surrendering.

The laugh she heard coming from Sebastian zipped up and down her spine before fading away. Reminding her again that perhaps accepting this assignment was not the wisest thing she'd ever done.

Chapter Eleven

Sebastian had no intention of actually eavesdropping. It just happened.

And it wasn't because he'd actually heard something that involved him, because he hadn't.

At least, not in the traditional sense.

What he wound up witnessing strongly involved him in an emotional sense, causing him to wonder—not for the first time—what if…?

All he'd initially intended was to pass by the living room. He'd been on his way to the kitchen to get himself something to eat. Brianna and her daughter had been in the house for a little more than a week now—long enough, apparently, for Carrie and Marilyn the cat to discover one another; the cat had seemingly "adopted" the four-year-old and followed her everywhere. And while there had been no awkward moments for any of them, he still found himself walking on eggshells, subconsciously wary of dislodging the careful balance of things.

Doing his very best not to stir up old memories, old feelings.

As if he could actually prevent them from finding him….

But Brianna didn't need to know that. Didn't need to know that there was this ache in his chest with her name on it, and every day it got a little bigger, grew a little more unwieldy and challenging.

Feeling this way, he had all the intention in the world to just keep walking by the living room, where he knew that his mother, Brianna and Carrie—with the cat in attendance—currently were. But then his attention was hijacked by the scenario he saw out of the corner of his eye.

A scenario involving his mother, Brianna and her daughter. Three separate generations rabidly involved in what looked like, from where he was standing, some sort of board game. Even the cat appeared to be part of it. Marilyn was kibitzing.

It was an old board game, from what he could actually see. He hadn't thought that anyone, especially children, played board games anymore. In today's sophisticated, high-tech electronic world, a simple board game seemed almost archaic.

Certainly outdated.

Yet there they were, his mother propped up on the

sofa with a mountain of pillows at her back, Brianna and Carrie gathered on the other side of the coffee table, deeply engrossed in something that looked suspiciously reminiscent of his old Monopoly game. The actual game board looked weathered enough to be his—he had no idea that his mother had kept it all these years.

He wouldn't even have looked into the room if it hadn't been for the laughter. That was what had first caught his attention. Not just Carrie's and Brianna's, but his mother's laughter as well.

It wasn't until *after* the sound had sunk in that he recognized it and subsequently realized that he hadn't heard that sound in a very long time.

He'd missed it.

Missed, too, not worrying about his mother, because ever since he'd taken that phone call, he'd been nothing *but* worried about his mother.

At least he'd lucked out by getting Brianna to come stay with her.

Brianna *and* her daughter, he amended.

He wasn't certain who was better for his mother. Brianna had a gentle, soothing way about her, but Carrie—Carrie was a whole different story. As Carrie and the cat had done, his mother and the little girl had hit it off instantly. Now his mother seemed to light up each time that Carrie came into the room.

It made him wonder—and just possibly harbor a sliver of yearning—what it would have been like if he'd married Brianna and started a family with her, giving his mother the grandchild she'd always longed for.

When she'd first mentioned that desire to him years ago, it had just seemed like the standard, humdrum request of every mother with adult children, and he'd just shrugged it off as such.

But now he could see just how strong that desire had to have actually been—and most likely still was—as he witnessed, time and again during this past week, how jubilant his mother became whenever she saw Carrie bounding toward her.

As if she was in the company of her own grandchild.

Sorry, Mom. I guess some things just weren't meant to be.

"Hey, what are you doing hovering over there?" Brianna called to him, breaking into his thoughts.

She'd been watching him beneath hooded eyes for a few minutes now and had given him what she felt was a decent amount of time to sneak away unnoticed if that was what he wanted. But Sebastian had remained where he was, a strange, almost wistful expression on his face.

Maybe he actually wanted to be called over, coaxed a little to join them. She certainly had no problem with that, with pretending that he had to have his arm twisted before he gave in. Having him join them might be great medicine for his mother, who, in her opinion, would really enjoy a nice domestic scene, complete with a family pet, all of them gathered around the coffee table.

So Brianna beckoned him over. "Come join us."

Time to go, Sebastian thought. "No, I'm actually on my way to—"

Although he pointed vaguely in the direction of the front door, which was definitely not the way he'd appeared to be heading, he came up empty. He hadn't counted on being put on the spot and thus had no excuse prepared to use for cover.

"To what?" Brianna challenged. "To go outside and peer in through the window to watch us play your old Monopoly game?"

He waved her off. "No. Really, you just continue doing what you're doing and I'll—"

He didn't get a chance to finish the half-formed excuse because Carrie had already gotten up, quickly crossed the room to get to his side and now had both her small hands wrapped around one of his. She looked as if she had every intention of literally dragging him into the living room and to the coffee table.

"Come," Carrie urged in a voice that sounded more like an order than just a soft plea. "Play Monopoly with us." She flashed a bright smile up at him. "I'm winning."

"Of course you are." He laughed. "I never had any doubts." Still, he tried to hold his ground against the little girl.

It wasn't going to happen, he realized almost immediately.

"But I promise I'll let you win if you come play the game with us," Carrie offered.

"Really, Sebastian, how can you possibly turn an offer like that down?" his mother asked him.

"Carrie hasn't learned how to take no for an answer yet," Brianna warned him, "so she's not about to politely back away or give up easily." She thought of what Sebastian had said to her when she'd first arrived. "And you haven't witnessed stubborn until you've had her wage a campaign against you," she told him, then added, "I'm afraid you're doomed, Sebastian."

Carrie, still holding on to his hand with both of hers and doing it as if she intended to hold on for dear life no matter how long it took, raised her brilliant blue eyes up to his and said what her mother referred to as the magic word. "Please?"

Sebastian knew he was probably just reading things into it, but the little girl made it sound as if her heart would break if he turned her down. And since he honestly had nothing planned and no particular place to go, he gave in.

"Sure, why not?" he said, allowing himself to be urged into the room.

He wasn't prepared for Carrie's enthusiastic cheer greeting his statement, nor was he prepared to see her gleefully leap up and down as if she was a pint-size cheerleader whose team had just scored a winning touchdown.

Neither was he prepared to have her tug on his arm and make him get down to her level.

When he did, she brushed her small lips against his cheek, her touch lighter than a butterfly landing on an orchid petal.

"Thank you," she said in a small, delicate voice that

made her momentarily sound a great deal younger than she normally did.

Sebastian *really* wasn't ready to have his heart utterly melt, just a moment before he served it up to the little girl on a silver platter.

Rising, he found he had to clear his throat. "Don't mention it," he murmured.

He pulled up a chair, taking the fourth side of the game board.

"I don't think I remember how to play," he admitted as he looked down at the board. A quick flash of a memory went by far too quickly for him to grab on to it and attempt to recall anything more.

A wave of nostalgia greeted him. It seemed to Sebastian as if the last time he'd sat just like this, contemplating this very game board, had been several decades ago.

"It'll come back to you," Brianna assured him. Her eyes met his for a brief moment and she added, "It's just like riding a bicycle. Or anything else you learned how to do on a regular basis."

Like love you?

The thought, coming in like a low-flying attack plane, startled him.

Why would it have even crossed his mind? As time had distanced him from his senior year, he had begun to doubt that what he'd felt for her then *had* been love. At least, not the forever kind. Maybe just the puppy-love variety.

That was what he'd told himself.

Seeing her at the reunion that night had stirred up

a lot of old feelings, reminding him of how it used to be. Of how he'd used to feel just being around her. But even so, he hadn't wanted to *actually* put a name to it, preferring that the emotion remain nameless until it had the good sense to fade away.

Obviously his subconscious had other ideas about it, because the nostalgia kept on coming back in insistent waves.

"You're probably right." He picked up one of the remaining pieces on the board. "Okay, let's get to it." He pushed his sleeves up his forearms. "Prepare to be dazzled, ladies." His game piece in his hand, he spared Carrie a glance. "And you don't have to 'let' me win. I can do it on my own, thanks."

Carrie's smile just stopped short of being smug. But the look on her face said she knew better but was so happy to see him play with them that she wasn't going to say anything, other than an enthusiastic "Okay!"

"Let the games begin," he declared, aware that all the markers had gone back to Go for a fresh game.

"I think," Sebastian said to Brianna a great many hours later, "you're raising a pint-size con artist. I can see her in Vegas in another seventeen years, being banned from all the casinos for card counting."

Brianna laughed as she cleaned up what had been an after-dinner round of cards. For such a small number of people, they certainly racked up an awful lot of dirty dishes and cups, she couldn't help thinking, bringing over another pile and putting them in the sink.

"I plan to make sure she only uses her powers for good," she told Sebastian. And then she paused for a moment, looking at Carrie. The powerhouse had finally just dozed off, refusing to miss a moment of what she assumed was an adult conversation: many words, few actual thoughts. "But she really does have a fantastic mind, doesn't she?"

Sebastian laughed and nodded his head. "All I know is that if she were my kid, I'd be studying every night just to try to stay ahead of her."

"I don't know how long I'd be able to keep that up," she told him. "She's already got a mind like a steel trap. It's like she remembers everything she sees, reads, learns—"

Sebastian looked at Brianna in disbelief. "She reads?"

Brianna smiled. It was so common in her life, she forgot that there were many who were fighting illiteracy. She needed to get back in the game.

"Like an old person. My father initially started to teach her. She was reading to *him* in less than two weeks. He's completely crazy about her." Brianna smiled fondly as she gazed down at the sleeping child. "She is rather hard to resist, as I think you might have found out today," she added drolly, referring to the games Carrie had corralled him into playing with them.

"A lot like her mother." Brianna laughed at that and then rolled her eyes. "What?" he asked, not seeing anything particularly funny about what he'd just said.

"Oh, please, don't even go there," she requested. The

man obviously needed a quick summary. "You *so* resisted me," she reminded him, but there was no bitterness or rancor in her voice, no look of recrimination when she glanced in his direction.

"About that…" Sebastian began hesitantly.

She raised her hand to stop whatever he was going to say. "It's okay. I didn't say that to make you feel guilty, or even to get you to apologize, or anything else along those lines. I just wanted to point out that I wasn't irresistible to you, no matter how you 'choose' to remember the past."

Instead of saying anything, Sebastian took hold of her wrist and drew her aside. He didn't want to have Carrie overhear them should she suddenly wake up. Glancing at her now, he wouldn't have put it past the little girl to feign sleeping just so that she could listen to them talk. She seemed to thoroughly enjoy being around adults rather than children her own age.

Brianna began to tug her hand away and found that, although his hold on her wrist felt relaxed, it was really quite strong. Her wrist was staying exactly where it was for the time being.

With a mental shrug, Brianna allowed him to take her over to one side of the room.

"What I 'choose' to remember," he said, keeping his voice low despite the distance now between them and the sleeping child, "is feeling hurt."

Now he wasn't making any sense at all. Brianna blinked, then stared at him, completely confused. What did *he* have to be hurt about? "What?"

"Hurt," he repeated for emphasis. "Because I had this big, romanticized dream, for lack of a better description, of the two of us going off to college and beginning our lives together. You and me against the world, that sort of corny thing," he admitted, growing more uncomfortable, not to mention hot. Who had taken out all the air from around here? "And then suddenly, you weren't part of that—you were telling me you weren't coming with me."

There was a reason for that and he *knew* it, she thought. "It wasn't exactly because I was going off on a month-long holiday touring Europe. I was staying home to take care of my injured father. My injured father who'd *almost died* in a car accident," she underscored, stunned that he had felt and thought that way.

"I know, I know, I was being an idiot. A self-centered, thoughtless, selfish idiot, but I'm just being honest about the way I felt at the time." He broke it down to just a few words. "I felt cheated and abandoned."

"Well, that made two of us," she retorted, doing her best *not* to revisit that time, because it always brought tears to her eyes.

"Yeah," he said, the emotion leaving his voice, "but you were the only one who actually had a right to those feelings. I am really sorry for leaving you to cope with everything on your own back then. I should have stayed to help you, to be supportive of you, and I didn't. I just thought about how you should have been there with me, not vice versa."

That he felt that way, that he was saying all the things

that had, at one time or another, crossed her mind, took the sting out of all the pain that she'd felt over the past ten years. She could be magnanimous now. She couldn't before.

"You had a degree to earn," she pointed out, her tone completely compassionate.

"So did you," he reminded her.

And if she could stay to help her father, he should have stayed to help her. With his mother ill now, he understood every emotion she had to have experienced, every emotion that had chosen to use her body for a battlefield. Since she'd come to them, she'd worked hard at being a pacifist.

"Yes," she agreed, but things had worked out in that area as well. "I was far more flexible about it than you could ever be. If you had stayed here with me, you would have felt I was holding you back, and things might not have gone well for us eventually."

"You mean compared to the way they actually have?" he asked with a touch of sarcasm.

"Compared to the way things actually did turn out," she amended tactfully. "You have a career you love, as do I, and I have a huge bonus on top of that. Had you stayed, then I would have never had Carrie come into my life. That little girl has opened up a brand-new world for me, Sebastian. She's made me a much better person," she confessed.

He looked at her for a long moment, new and old feelings all crowding together in his chest, bringing a host of memories and whispers of the past with them.

He pushed them to one side, not having enough time to sift through them now.

"Not possible," he told Brianna.

"But she did," she insisted. "Carrie has made me a—"

He touched her face then, lightly skimming his fingertips along her cheek. Remembering that old feeling of how his day hadn't actually started until he saw her. "You can't improve on perfection," he whispered.

"Now you're just making fun of me," Brianna protested.

"No," Sebastian told her just before he gave in to the overwhelming yearning that ate him alive from the inside out and brought his mouth down on hers. "I'm not."

Chapter Twelve

Nothing had changed.

And everything had changed.

Sebastian's kiss still had the power to set her pulse racing, to set desire exploding in her veins, swiftly growing and wiping out every thought in her head. *That* part hadn't changed.

But life in general, *their* lives in general, had changed enormously. They had changed in focus, progressed and moved on. Brianna had worked tirelessly to help her father regain the use of his legs, had in effect brought his soul back from the dead. In the interim, she'd gone on to become a nurse as well as kept his store open and running until he was able to resume working there, something that had taken the better part of more than three years.

And, as if that wasn't enough, after that she had also taken on the mind-staggering responsibility of being a single parent and raising her late fiancé's daughter as her own.

As for him, he'd gone on to get his degree, then had restructured his life and moved to Japan, where he was currently putting his skills to use.

Neither one of them was the optimistic and eager teenager on the brink of tomorrow, as they'd been ten years ago. And yet, the essence of those people, those dreamers, was buried deep inside of each of them and had somehow reconnected with this simple, albeit inflaming, pressing of lips.

Unable to pull away, Sebastian tightened his arms around her as he deepened the kiss, deepened it to the point that there was no viable way out for him. Without realizing it, he'd hit the point of no return, at least in this instance, and discovered that Brianna still had a way of speaking to his soul, of making him think of nothing else but her.

Want nothing else but her.

What was to have been just a very simple kiss steeped in nostalgia was anything *but* simple. It made him remember the one night that had, all those years ago, seemed like the beginning of everything. He hadn't realized at the time, a scant few hours before they'd found out about her father's car accident, that it also marked the end of their time together.

Her heart pounding, Brianna threaded her fingers

through his hair. She'd always loved the feel of his thick, silky hair. Her head reeling, she leaned into the kiss.

Leaned into him.

Even as she did, she told herself that this was only going to lead to heartache, but that small voice of logic was getting weaker.

Her desire was blotting out all resistance.

Any moment now, she would throw caution to the winds and allow him to take her to his room. To take her where they were inevitably going.

Where she desperately *wanted* to go.

Everything had changed.

And yet, nothing had changed, because her feelings for him hadn't changed.

"Mama?"

Like a thin, sharp blade, the tiny, almost inaudible voice effectively pierced what had, until just now, felt like an impenetrably thick, clear bubble.

Startled, Brianna practically sprang back, not knowing what she was going to say. Dazed, disoriented, she swiftly tried to clear her head so that she would be able to give Carrie a coherent answer to whatever her daughter was going to ask.

"Yes, honey?"

Dear God, her voice was all but shaking—just like the rest of her. Was that because of her daughter, or because she realized that Sebastian's kiss had opened up the door to a room she had promised herself had been sealed shut?

Carrie looked from her to Sebastian, a puzzled expression on her small, oval-shaped face. "Are we going somewhere again?"

Brianna exchanged glances with Sebastian. He was as mystified as she was.

She turned toward her daughter. "No, honey, we're not going anywhere for a while. What makes you think that we are?"

"Because you're kissing Sebastian goodbye," she said innocently.

"Your mom wasn't kissing me goodbye, Carrie. She was just thanking me," Sebastian told the little girl without hesitating.

Brianna looked at him, amazed at how easily the excuse had flowed from his tongue. Did lying come easily to him these days, or was he just trying to cover for her and set the little girl's mind at ease?

She wasn't sure which it was and it just reminded her that, for the most part, the man standing before her was really a stranger. He'd had the past ten years to become one.

Carrie gazed up at him, clearly confused. Rubbing the sleep from her eyes, she stretched a little, then asked him, "What was Mama thanking you for?"

This time, there was a short pause. Was he waiting for her to come up with something? Because right now, her mind was a complete blank.

And then she heard Sebastian tell Carrie, "Because I told her that I was going to go get a pizza for dinner tomorrow night. Your mom told me how much you like pizza and I do, too." Sebastian sat down beside Carrie on the sofa.

The little girl beamed. "What kind of pizza?" she asked.

Instead of answering, he asked her a question. "What's your favorite?"

"Pepperoni and sausage," Carrie piped up, wiggling her feet in anticipation of sinking her teeth into a slice.

"No kidding," Sebastian marveled. "That's my favorite, too."

His words earned him another wide, all-inclusive grin from the four-year-old.

Brianna knew for a fact that his favorite toppings consisted of four different cheeses and no meat.

Nice save, she mouthed over her daughter's head, impressed with his quick thinking.

She also appreciated his being so thoughtful of Carrie. The little girl had really taken to him. Carrie had been just an infant when her father had died and Brianna always regretted the fact that Carrie was going to grow up with no memory of either of her biological parents. For a short duration, Carrie would see what it was like having a father figure in her life.

Turning toward Carrie, Brianna announced, "It's time to get you to bed, pumpkin."

Carrie appeared crestfallen. "Do I have to go to bed right now, Mama? Can't I stay up for a few more minutes?"

It was hard not giving in to the child. Every day, Brianna had to fight her own inclination to spoil her and let her have her own way. Enforcing a few rules was for her daughter's own good.

"It's already past your bedtime, Carrie," she said as sternly as possible.

"I was asleep before my bedtime, so can I have that time back now?" Carrie asked without even missing a beat.

Sebastian could only stare at her, blown away by her reasoning process. He shook his head as if to clear his own brain.

"I'd start saving up for her college tuition *now* if I were you. This kid has the makings of a really *great* legal mind," he predicted.

Brianna laughed as she gathered Carrie up into her arms. Like a little monkey, Carrie scrambled over to one side, resting against her hip bone. Holding her with one arm, Brianna stroked Carrie's hair with her free hand. "Carrie just likes to argue."

The remark made Sebastian smile. "Like I said, a great legal mind."

"Can Sebastian tuck me in?" Carrie asked suddenly.

Her daughter was just trying to stall, Brianna thought.

"Carrie, you can't just assume someone is at your beck and call just because you want him to be," she pointed out, looking for a way to keep Carrie's feelings from being hurt while extricating Sebastian from what seemed like an awkward situation.

But the one thing Brianna already knew was that you couldn't extricate someone if they really didn't want to be extricated.

And Sebastian obviously didn't.

"I'd love to tuck you in," Sebastian said.

Carrie beamed triumphantly. Her small, sweetheart chin rose up just a tad as she bragged, "See, Mama, Sebastian said he'd love to. That means he's okay with tucking me in."

Sebastian's warm chocolate eyes shifted over to look at Brianna. "I'm sorry. Did I just wind up undoing years of discipline?"

From the dreamy expression in Carrie's eyes, Brianna could only deduce that her daughter had just developed her very first crush. She could only shake her head in response to his question.

"Something like that." She laughed, dismissing the apology. "Don't worry about it. The bottom line is the same as it's always been—that she's happy."

"I think that's safe to assume at the moment," he replied, looking at Carrie.

Because the little girl opened up her arms to him, Sebastian stepped forward to take her from Brianna. "If it's okay with you," he prefaced.

"Sure, be my guest," Brianna told him. "You want to carry her up the stairs, go right ahead."

"She weighs less than a feather," Sebastian said as he took Carrie from her.

"I weigh more than a feather," Carrie protested. "More than a *sack* of feathers," she insisted.

"A *small* sack of feathers," he allowed, easily carrying her up the stairs. "Are you happy, Carrie?" he asked, deliberately keeping a serious expression on his face as he asked.

"Uh-huh," she answered immediately, tightening her small arms around his neck.

He hadn't expected to feel something tugging on his heart just now, hadn't expected to experience a strange, bittersweet feeling in response to the exceedingly simple, uncalculated action. He was beginning to understand what the expression "wrapped around her little finger" was all about. He was wrapped around Carrie's—and he didn't even mind.

"Your bottom line's been met," he told Brianna. "Carrie says she's happy."

"Yes," Brianna acknowledged, "I heard."

Entering the room Carrie shared with her mother, he placed her on the queen-size bed.

"Now tuck me in," Carrie told him, patiently waiting for him to comply.

"Like this?" he asked, taking the edge of the blanket and bringing it to cover her up to her chin.

Carrie wiggled up higher in her bed, moving so that the blanket was a little farther down. "Very good," she pronounced as if she were a teacher and he the student.

"Okay, then, good night," he said to her, beginning to back away.

"What about my story?" she asked, stopping him in his tracks.

"What story?" he wanted to know.

"You're supposed to read me a bedtime story," she informed him. Then, in case he didn't know that she could read, Carrie told him, "I can read it myself, but I fall asleep faster if someone else reads it to me."

This was getting out of hand, Brianna thought, stepping forward. Carrie was stalling. The little girl obviously had a crush. While she could totally understand why Carrie felt that way, she didn't want Sebastian to feel obligated to sit by her bedside and read to her. That went way above and beyond the call of duty.

"I'd run while running is still an option if I were you," she advised. "I'll read to Carrie."

But rather than thank her for coming to his rescue, Sebastian pretended as if he hadn't heard her. Instead, he said to Carrie, "I'd love to read to you. What story would you like to hear?"

Carrie didn't need to hear any more. Scrambling out of bed, she made a beeline for the shelves where her books were housed. After selecting one conveniently located on the bottom shelf, Carrie handed the eight-by-eleven illustrated storybook to Sebastian, then dashed back into bed.

Pulling the covers up to her chin, she happily declared, "Ready!"

Sebastian could feel Brianna looking at him. He wasn't sure if she was waiting for him to begin reading—or to bolt. He wasn't about to do the latter. For reasons he didn't fully comprehend, the idea of reading a bedtime story to an eager audience of one pleased him.

Settling into a chair, he opened the book, then glanced in Brianna's direction.

"Why don't you kick back a little?" he suggested.

There was no reason for her to hang around. He certainly knew how to read a story to a child. "You've more than earned it."

Kick back. Easy for him to say, Brianna thought. She felt so tense right now. The worst part was that she could hardly think straight. But there was no sense in arguing with him about this.

She paused by the doorway. "You're sure you're okay with this?" she asked.

"Very sure," he assured her, then waved her out. "Go. Eat something decadent. Watch something on TV. Read that book you haven't had a chance to crack open. Go," he repeated, motioning her away just before he opened up the book that Carrie had given him. Leaning back in the chair, he began to read.

Brianna forced herself to cross the threshold and walk out of the room. Sebastian was fully capable of tackling the story about the goings-on of one of Carrie's favorite cast of characters. There were seven "Bear" books in the small library that Carrie had amassed. To the best of her recollection, her daughter had selected one from the middle of the pile.

Well, he asked for it, Brianna thought as she made her way down the stairs. She had no idea what to do with the free time she'd been awarded. Every minute of her day had been booked for so long, she was at a loss how to spend unscheduled time.

When in doubt, fall back on your routine, she counseled herself.

So she went to check on Sebastian's mother and

found that the older woman had dozed off watching TV in her room. Brianna's first impulse was to turn off the set, draw the covers over the sleeping woman and shut the light just as she tiptoed out of the room.

But she knew from experience that those simple actions might actually wake up the woman. With that in mind, Brianna lowered the volume on the TV and dimmed the lights only slightly.

She made her way into the kitchen next. She washed the dishes by hand and then tidied up. Finished, she looked around for a moment, regarding the fruits of her labor.

It was at that point that she decided that she'd had enough of "free time." She went back upstairs to check on Carrie and Sebastian in her room.

If nothing else, Brianna was fairly confident that Sebastian was just about ready to be rescued. Granted, he'd volunteered, but that was before he had a clue what he was getting himself into. Carrie was not a child who merely listened docilely.

If a word was skipped, she knew it and asked to have the passage reread. If it was a new story—which this wasn't—there were questions to ask, motivations to explore. Like the inquiring mind that she was, Carrie wanted to understand what she was listening to, no matter how long it took to explain everything.

Brianna quietly approached the room, then very slowly eased open the door that she'd deliberately left ajar. She heard Sebastian's voice, strong and animated, still reading the story to her daughter.

What she *didn't* hear was Carrie questioning anything or offering her comments to Sebastian about the story in general.

That was because, she now saw, the little girl had apparently fallen asleep.

Well, *that* had certainly happened in record time, she silently marveled, easing the door open the rest of the way.

Catching the movement of the door out of the corner of his eye, Sebastian stopped reading and looked up. Seeing Brianna in the doorway, he smiled and mouthed, "Hi."

Then, glancing at Carrie one more time to assure himself that she was really asleep, Sebastian quietly closed the storybook, set it aside on the nightstand and eased himself out of the chair.

Sebastian said nothing as he left the room, afraid that the slightest sound might wake the little girl. But once the door was closed and he'd moved a few feet down the hall, away from the room, he looked at Brianna and smiled.

It was the same kind of slightly crooked smile that had initially captured her heart all those years ago in math class.

"Mission accomplished," he told her with a smart salute. "She's sound asleep."

"I'd give it a little while longer before I said that," Brianna advised. "Carrie has a way of suddenly popping up like toast even if you think she's out like the proverbial light. By the way, your mother is asleep, too."

"That sounds good. The more rest she gets, the faster she'll recover," he reasoned. "Well, I've got nothing planned for the rest of the evening," he told her. "How about you?"

"I've washed the dishes and tidied up, so, no, I don't have anything else planned."

"You *plan* washing dishes?" he asked.

"I don't like going to bed unless everything's cleaned up."

"So you're going to bed?" he asked.

"Eventually," she allowed. "Why? What do you have in mind?"

He thought it best not to share that right now. Instead, he asked, "How about a movie?"

"As long as we can watch it here," she qualified.

"Definitely," he answered. "I'll make the popcorn. You pick the movie," he told her.

Suddenly, she wasn't tired anymore. And the tension she'd been harboring decreased by at least several notches. For now.

"You're on," she told him.

Chapter Thirteen

Brianna realized that she'd been holding her breath through at least half the movie that she'd selected for them to watch. It was an action thriller, but her lack of oxygen intake had nothing to do with the excitement on the screen and everything to do with the untapped excitement sitting fewer than two feet away from her on the sofa.

She kept thinking that Sebastian was just biding his time, waiting to make his move when she was least prepared for it. After all, there'd been blatant signals that he was leaning that way earlier. There'd been definite indications that if Carrie went on sleeping after she had been safely carried off to bed, Brianna and Sebastian would find themselves in his room.

In his bed.

Just the way they had that night when his mother had gone out of town to take care of his sick great-aunt. The night of the prom.

Brianna had to admit that, despite the fact that she had picked the movie, she was only half paying attention to it. But when the credits rolled, the closest she and Sebastian had come to even casually touching one another was when they had both reached for the popcorn at the same time, and she decided that maybe it was time to stop holding her breath.

It was obvious that the long, toe-curling kiss they'd shared earlier was *not* a preview of things to come. Instead, it just happened and was destined to stand apart from anything else that might go on between them.

You're supposed to be relieved, Bree. You don't want to lose your heart to him all over again, remember? This time, you know there's no future for the two of you. He'll be leaving for Japan again and you'll be staying here, with your child and your father and that career you've hammered out for yourself.

And then, like an annoying mantra, the voice in her head added, *It never goes well for you when your heart's involved. You know that.*

Brianna blinked. The TV screen in front of them had gone blank. She could feel Sebastian silently looking at her.

"What?" she asked, afraid he'd said something and she'd been so engrossed in her own thoughts that she'd missed it.

"You didn't like the movie." It wasn't a question, but

a verdict, delivered with obvious disappointment. "We could have watched something else."

"No, I liked the movie," Brianna protested, contradicting him.

"You didn't say anything," he pointed out. "Generally, when you watch something, you do a running commentary." At least, she used to, he silently amended.

Brianna laughed quietly. "Not anymore. Carrie doesn't like me to talk while she's watching something, and since she's become my 'viewing buddy,' I've learned to hold my tongue."

"So I have her to thank?" He grinned. "The girl's definitely a genius. I never thought *anything* could get you to hold your tongue and keep from expressing your opinion," he marveled with more fondness than he'd intended.

"I don't know whether to laugh or be insulted," she quipped.

"It wasn't meant to be insulting," he told her. "If anything, it was meant as an affectionate observation." Picking up the remote control, he aimed it toward the set and shut off the TV, then turned so that he was facing her. He found himself hungry for the sound of her voice, to just talk the way they used to. "You've done a terrific job with her. How long have you been raising her?"

"Almost from the beginning. She was thirteen months old when J.T. was killed. I'm the only parent she's ever known." Which struck her as ironic, since she really wasn't Carrie's parent at all, at least not biologically.

"Her mother died in childbirth," she said, aware that she'd already told him that earlier.

"Childbirth?" When she'd initially told him, he hadn't really paid all that much attention to the information, but now he did and he had to admit the thought surprised him. "I didn't think that sort of thing happened anymore."

Unfortunately, the circumstances were against Carrie's mother. "It does if the mother starts hemorrhaging and there's no doctor around."

"No doctor?" he echoed. "What kind of a hospital was she in?"

Brianna laughed shortly, shaking her head. "That was just the problem—she wasn't. Carrie's mother didn't like doctors. Instead, she had a midwife in attendance. Most of the time, that's great and midwives are pretty sharp. But, by some fluke, this one was out of her depth, especially since there were complications right from the beginning."

She could see the whole scenario unfolding in her mind's eye. J.T.'s frantic call to her for help. By the time she'd arrived, the paramedics were already there—and unable to help. The young woman was already dead. She'd stayed the night, taking care of the newborn while trying to keep J.T. calm. He'd been there to help her through her father's blackest days, and she thought it only fair to try to return the favor.

"J.T. blamed himself for her death because he hadn't insisted on a doctor. If his wife had been in a hospital, she might still be alive today. And so would he," she added.

Sebastian wasn't following her logic. "How do you figure the last part?" he asked. "You said he died in a boating accident."

She sighed heavily. She should have been able to get J.T. through his emotional turmoil, but she'd failed. And that would always be on her. "It's way too easy to have an accident if you're driving a craft under the influence."

"He was drinking?"

Brianna raised one shoulder in a vague shrug. "For the most part, he'd stopped. That was part of the conditions of our engagement," she admitted, "that he get his drinking under control. But J.T. couldn't quite put his demons to rest and that weekend was his late wife's birthday. He used to say that he drank to numb the pain and the emptiness."

Her mouth curved in an ironic smile. "The evening we got engaged, he told me that *I* helped numb his pain and fill the emptiness. I guess I just wasn't strong enough for the job that Saturday when he set sail. It was the last time I saw him alive." Brianna looked down at her ring finger on her left hand. It was empty now. She'd switched the engagement ring J.T. had given her to her right hand, a constant reminder of the promise that wasn't fulfilled. "We'd been engaged all of three weeks when he died."

Sebastian was trying to pull the pieces together in an attempt to focus his mind on something other than the fact that he wanted to hold her and make her smile again. A *real* smile this time.

"I thought you said the boating accident occurred a week before the wedding."

"It did," she said. "J.T. was in a hurry to get married. I think he was hoping that I'd make his nightmares go away. Guess I didn't do such a hot job," she concluded quietly.

"Don't you dump this on yourself," Sebastian chided her. He knew she had that tendency. For some reason, she felt it was her job to save the world. For as long as he'd known her, she'd always gravitated toward animals and people who needed saving.

He supposed that, in a way, he fell into that group himself.

"You weren't his keeper," he insisted.

"No," she agreed halfheartedly, "but I was his friend as well as his fiancée. I should have realized that weekend was going to be extra-difficult for him to get through. I should have been there for him instead of opting to keep the store running while he went out."

She shook her head at her own naïveté. "I honestly thought getting away with his friends was going to be good for J.T. You know, a bunch of guys blowing off steam, telling fish stories, things like that." And then she added more softly, "I had a gut feeling, but I didn't pay any attention to it. I thought that if I said anything to him at the last minute about not going, it would have sounded too controlling. So I opted to help Dad in the store and take care of Carrie while he had fun.

"Except that he didn't have fun," she said more to herself than to Sebastian. "The medical examiner said he had twice the legal limit of alcohol in his blood when he died."

"And his friends?" he prodded, wondering why one of them hadn't taken over when they saw that J.T. was in no shape to pilot the craft.

There'd been no help in that quarter, she thought. "According to the M.E., they had all been drinking. The coast guard managed to recover all the bodies," she said, almost as if she was reading an account of the accident out loud.

"No survivors?" Sebastian asked sympathetically.

Brianna shook her head, momentarily unable to answer him. Tears had filled her throat, all but swelling it shut.

Seeing her expression, Sebastian wordlessly slipped his arm around her shoulders and drew her closer to him. His only intent was to offer her some sort of comfort if he could.

"God, but you've had a rough time of it," he told her. A lesser person would have probably crumbled by now, undone by the sheer weight of all the events she'd had to deal with.

Brianna drew in a breath slowly, pulled herself together and then shrugged carelessly in response to his comment.

"People have had it a lot rougher," she told him, refusing to allow herself to slip into a self-pitying mode. She'd been there several times in her life and found that if she gave in to it long enough, it sucked her spirit out of her, leaving her utterly dry. She knew that that would completely destroy her.

So instead, she forced herself to rise above it, to rally as best she could. She'd always been an upbeat person in the long run, and she knew that a positive attitude was the only thing that could see her through the dark times.

"Besides, I've had a lot of good things happen to me, too. My dad survived his accident and he's absolutely fully recovered—"

"Thanks to you," Sebastian pointed out.

She refused to take credit for that. "I couldn't have gotten him to do anything he really didn't want to do." She summarized her part in all this in a few modest words. "I just figured out which of his buttons to press, that's all."

"That wasn't the way I heard the story," Sebastian informed her.

She looked at him, curious. "From who?"

"My mother. She made a point of keeping tabs on you and your father, and then sent me lengthy reports about what was going on."

She had always gotten along with his mother, but when her father was involved in that accident, she'd turned all her attention to making him get well. She'd stopped interacting with anyone else on a regular basis for literally *months*.

"Did you ask her to?" she asked.

He looked at her for a long moment. "I really want to say yes here, but I won't lie to you. She did that all on her own. I think at the time she was still hoping that you and I would...well, you know," he said, not wanting to put either one of them on the spot, or make them uncomfortable by saying the last part out loud.

A sad, resigned smile curved the corners of her mouth. "Yes, I know."

She also knew that if she continued sitting here talking to him about the past, she would wind up giving in to the strong feelings stirring within her, emotions that still belonged to Sebastian alone. It would be a great deal more prudent, not to mention wiser, for her to take her leave now—while she still could.

She began to get up as she made the obligatory excuses. "Well, it's late and I told your mother I wanted to start her on a very light exercise regimen tomorrow, so I'd better be heading up to bed."

Her little speech delivered, she expected to go. But as she turned to leave, Sebastian caught her wrist in his hand.

When she looked at him quizzically, he said, "I'm sorry, Bree."

His words hit her right smack in her chest. She pretended to ignore the sensation vibrating through her. It would only act against her.

"We've already been through this, Sebastian," she told him quietly. "And I said that you've got nothing to be sorry for."

"Yes, I do," he contradicted her. "A whole slew of things to be sorry for. Most of all, I'm sorry that I let you go."

As she recalled, *he* was the one who had gone, not her. "You make it sound as if I was a pet deer you had tethered in a cage and decided to release one morning." His wording left a little something to be desired. "You know, for an English professor, you don't exactly have a way with words sometimes."

Rather than take exception, Sebastian inclined his head, conceding the point. "That's because those are the times when I'm emotionally invested and afraid of saying the wrong thing."

She would have been willing to bet anything that he was anything *but* emotionally invested right now.

"Okay," she allowed, stretching out the word as she tried to understand exactly what he *thought* he was telling her. "In any case, I forgive you."

But as she tried to get up for a second time, she found that Sebastian was still holding on to her wrist. Resigned, she sank back down onto the sofa. "Anything else?"

"As a matter of fact, yes," he answered.

"All right, what?" she asked when he didn't immediately follow up his words with anything further and the moments began to tick away.

"This." He said it so quietly, there was a part of her that thought that maybe they were communicating by telepathy rather than with words. Supposedly, some people in love could do that.

Except that they *weren't* people in love.

Brianna caught her breath as his hand lightly skimmed along her throat. The caress branded her skin.

He tilted her head just a fraction and then, in the next moment, his lips brushed against hers so incredibly softly she was sure she was just imagining it. That she had all but willed it with her mind.

But she hadn't.

And the next moment, the first kiss was followed by another.

And another.

Each flowering kiss was a little more forceful, a little lengthier than the last.

By the fourth kiss, rockets went off in her head and a hunger was suddenly unleashed within her, a hunger that she had never experienced before, even when she'd been on the brink of making love with him that very first time.

The hunger was coupled with fear—fear that he would pull back.

And then he did and she felt a desperation taking hold, interweaving itself with a sense of bereavement.

"You'd better go upstairs," he told her hoarsely. When she merely looked at him as if she didn't understand what he was saying, he repeated the sentence, saying the words more forcefully. "Go. I don't know how much longer I can hold back."

"Maybe I don't want you to hold back," she told him, remaining exactly where she was, her lips hardly moving. The only part moving was her heart, which had gone back to pounding wildly, the way it had initially.

"You don't know what you're saying, Bree."

Her eyes held his as she remembered their past and

remembered, too, what she had once thought would be their future.

"I know *exactly* what I'm saying," she told him, her voice just a hint above a whisper. "Don't worry," she added, never taking her eyes off his. "No strings, no requests for promises. All I want is tonight. Just now," she told him, her breath warm on his lips as she spoke.

Seducing him.

Taking the last of his willpower and breaking it into tiny bits.

"Oh, damn, Bree," he lamented, "you're making it hard to walk away."

"Then don't," she suggested softly. "Don't."

He could feel the last of his resolve being blown to pieces as he pulled her back into his arms. As he kissed her with all the pent-up emotion he had. But now it was out, exploding right before him and ensnaring him just as much as it ensnared her.

It was as if, after years of separation, he'd been allowed to glimpse his soul again.

The intense desire to reunite, to become one, to become whole again, was just too overwhelming to resist.

So he didn't.

Chapter Fourteen

"Wait."

The hoarsely voiced entreaty came from Brianna.

She'd summoned the last of her all but shredded resolve in an attempt to momentarily pause the wild rush that had seized not only her, but she suspected him as well. She needed him to listen to her, provided she could still string a few words together.

Sebastian felt more than heard her asking him to hold off. His pulse hammering against his rib cage, he forced himself to pull back.

It was far from easy, but he wasn't some sort of rutting pig. "You changed your mind."

It wasn't a question but, to him, an agonized statement of fact. At the last minute, her senses had obviously returned to her. The realization created an ache deep in the pit of his stomach.

Paradise lost before it was gained, he thought with a heavy heart, resigned to his fate.

Brianna took his words to be a question and answered him with breathless feeling. "Oh, hell no. I haven't changed my mind, and don't you dare change yours."

He looked at her, confused. "Then why—?"

Brianna didn't expect him to think along the same lines that she did. After all, he hadn't had to constantly place the needs of a little girl above his own for the past three years. She'd been doing it ever since she'd become first Carrie's legal guardian and then her adoptive parent. It was second nature to her.

Even so, it was a struggle to think clearly. All she wanted was to make love with Sebastian. To feel his hands along her body, to finally, *finally* become one with him again.

Her mouth dry, she managed to push out the words and actually sound as if she was making some sort of sense.

"We need to go to your room to do this," she told him. "If either Carrie or your mother comes out of their bedrooms for any reason—"

She didn't need to finish. He understood.

"Right, right," he agreed wholeheartedly, already on his feet. Holding her hand, he drew her up with him as well. Ready to all but sprint up the stairs, Sebastian still paused for a moment. He threaded his fingers through her hair so that he could turn her face up to his. And then he kissed her. Soundly.

Dazed, her head spinning, she looked at Sebastian the moment he drew his lips away from hers.

"What was that for?" she asked breathlessly.

"For not saying no," he told her. The next second, he laced his fingers through hers and was drawing her over to the stairs.

Brianna smiled to herself. How could she say no to him when everything inside her was screaming yes?

The door to Sebastian's bedroom closed.

Finally.

More than ever, she was anxious for his touch, for the feel of his firm, capable hands moving along her skin. Caressing her.

Making love with her.

Clothes flew off their bodies in a flurry of material, falling to the rug, comingling with little to no notice paid to what had fallen where. Clothes didn't matter.

Only *this* mattered.

How had he let this happen? This separation that had kept them apart for so long, that had scissored through their happiness, leaving only rubble and ruin?

The question hammered away at his brain. How could he have allowed hurt feelings to drive a wedge between the two of them?

He needed to know because he'd turned his back on this. He had to have been crazy, he concluded. Crazy to leave her, crazy to maintain distance between them.

Crazy not to attempt to get back in contact with her for all those years.

Years he wasn't going to get back.

Years, despite this frenzy-driven interlude, that he might not be able to trade for something positive on the other side of this night.

Sebastian was no longer a dreamer. He'd long since become grounded in reality and that reality wouldn't allow him to be foolish enough to believe in a different life. He and Brianna had let too much time pass, had too much happen to each of them individually to just murmur, "Never mind," and pick up where they had left off ten years ago.

He knew all this to be true, that it all mattered—but not at this moment.

Now he just needed to immerse himself in her, to absorb her, to drink her in as if she were a tall, frosty glass of water and he had just spent ten years crawling through the desert. He only wanted to feel, think and exist in the moment with her.

And nothing else mattered.

It was a madness in the blood and he knew it, but he didn't care.

As he once again sought her mouth—the very reason for his existence on this earth at this moment—they were suddenly tumbling onto his king-size bed, their limbs tangling, their body parts instantly heating at even the barest hint of contact.

There wasn't a single microinch of his body that didn't throb from wanting her.

Sebastian tried to be as gentle as he could, restraining his all but overwhelming sense of urgency, as he ran his hands all over her body.

Unable to satisfy himself.

Unable to get enough of her.

The quest for more seemed as if it were never ending. And that was the way he wanted it.

Because he didn't want this to end.

His mouth followed the path forged by his hands and he gloried in the fact that Brianna twisted and turned beneath him, arching to absorb every sensation, every delicate nuance.

Brianna felt as if she were running in some endless marathon, unable to catch her breath.

At the same time she was struggling very hard not to emit a cry that would pierce the stillness of the night and quite possibly garner them an unwanted audience of two.

At the very least, it could wake up either his mother or her daughter—if not both—and cause questions to be born full-grown and viable in the wake of the noise.

Brianna was well aware of the danger of crying out, knew that it could very possibly terminate this wild, adrenaline-fueled ride she found herself on. But it was *so* hard to contain the sound of pure, raw, guttural pleasure broken down to its basic components that was throbbing in her throat, begging for release.

She wasn't sure just how much longer she could control herself.

And then it came to her, the only way she knew of to keep from all but shrieking out her enjoyment.

Throwing Sebastian off balance, she deftly switched positions so that suddenly, *she* was the one on top, *she* was the one with the upper hand.

Straddling him now that he was under her, she began to weave a tapestry of soft, openmouthed kisses along his upper torso.

She artfully applied her tongue as well and slowly worked her way down, past his chest, past his waist. Past his navel.

She paused in her impromptu, erotic trail blazing long enough to lightly blow a small cloud of warm air along the lower region of his body.

Just as she'd hoped, she was instantly rewarded with visual evidence that Sebastian was indeed responding to this exquisite torture.

When she heard a strangled groan escape his lips, she knew he was all but at the breaking point.

As was she.

With a triumphant laugh, she hovered a moment longer, seductively teasing him with her tongue just along his hipline. Her heart racing, she slid her way up along the length of his body until their faces were on the same level again.

As she reached down to caress him, he caught her wrist in his hand, holding her still.

"Where did you learn to torture a man this way?" he asked in a barely audible whisper.

"I didn't 'learn' it anywhere," she answered innocently. "It's just creative instinct."

The next moment, raising his head, Sebastian seized her mouth, covering it with his own, and then, as he tasted her surrender, his arms surrounding her, he flipped their positions, reversing them so that once again she found herself under him.

Under him and utterly compliant.

He drew his head back for a second, looked into her eyes and knew—knew she was ready. Knew she was his for the taking.

Which was good, because he didn't think he could hold himself in check even a split second longer.

He took Brianna's mouth again, his pulse racing with each kiss. Echoes of the past tightly surrounded him as he parted her legs with his knee and then drove himself into her as if his very life depended on this union.

Because right now, it did.

They'd been here, just like this, once before. And yet...

And yet it felt all brand-new.

This joining enticed him like a temptress who had been waiting all eternity for this moment.

A wild frenzy rose up in his veins, a frenzy born in the wake of Brianna's frantic movements beneath him.

Born in the barely contained, barely muffled cries of absolute pleasure he tasted as her mouth continued to be sealed to his.

The frenzy continued to grow, feeding on the way her hips were pressed to his, even as they were arching, bucking, moving only slightly less quickly than the wings of a hummingbird hovering in a single position.

He felt her fingers digging into his shoulders, felt her nails scraping against his flesh.

The sharp pain was muted, its edge all but completely blotted out in the wake of the explosions going on inside him.

They reached the very tip of the known universe and then, after hovering there for what seemed like an endless moment, they went into a free fall, their hands, bodies and souls joined.

Sebastian felt that at any second, his heart would crack through his rib cage and make a break for freedom, still pounding insanely.

Instinctively, his arms tightened around Brianna's damp body. At first protectively, and then in fear. Fear that as the moment grew further and further away, so would she.

More exhausted than he'd ever thought humanly possible, Sebastian still managed to turn his head and press a kiss to what he hoped was the top of her forehead.

But he couldn't swear to the accuracy of his delivery, only to the fact that Brianna had stolen not only his breath—and possibly his stamina—but his heart as well.

How can she steal what she already had? his brain taunted him.

In a moment of complete clarity, Sebastian suddenly realized why he'd never been in another relationship after they'd parted company. Because, together or apart, Brianna still retained possession of his heart.

And what good did that do him? he silently demanded. He hadn't had any contact with her after he'd left for college. No contact whatsoever. Instead, he'd allowed his ego, his baseless pride, to dictate his course of action—or lack thereof—and doom him to an existence filled with professional accomplishment yet devoid of any sort of emotional connections.

For all the people that were always around him in Tokyo, he was soul-wrenchingly alone.

"So," he heard her say, invading his thought process, "same time, same place, ten years from now?"

He turned his head to look at her, certain he hadn't heard her correctly. "What?"

"Same time, same place, ten years from now?" she repeated. When the confused expression on his face didn't recede, she patiently pointed out, "We made love here, in your bed like this, the night of the prom."

She didn't have to add what she was leaving unsaid: that they'd made love for the very first time just before the hospital had called on her cell phone to tell her that her father had been involved in a near-fatal accident and that they weren't entirely sure if he would make it through the night.

"Did we?" He asked in such an innocent voice, it was her turn to stare at him.

"You don't remember?" she asked him, trying not to sound as stunned as she felt.

And then he smiled at her, that soft, bone-melting

smile that always got to her. "I don't remember anything that happened before we came up to this room
and then went on to systematically destroy the world
as we once knew it."

"Oh, you're kidding," she realized, feeling a wave of
absolutely stunning relief.

For a second, she'd believed his performance and
had actually thought that Sebastian didn't remember
their first time the way she did. For her, that first interlude between them was forever embossed on her brain
as well as her heart. That it was, in some measure, embossed on his as well meant a great deal to her.

"No," he told her in utter seriousness, "I'm not kidding." He cupped her cheek just before he kissed her
softly on the lips. "It *does* feel as if we just forged our
own brand-new world."

She smiled up at him, then rested her head on his
shoulder as she curled her body up against his.

"That was very poetic," she said with a contented
sigh.

She allowed herself just a few more minutes to savor
this dreamlike state. All too soon, the peace she was
experiencing would break up like the bubbles hovering
above a bubble bath. She knew that this contentment's
life expectancy was incredibly short. Almost over before it began. That didn't seem very fair.

"Where do we go from here?"

The question suddenly escaped his lips, even though
he'd already thought that through logically and knew
there was no final satisfactory destination for them.

She raised her head and looked at him. "Do we have to decide that right now?" she asked, lightly grazing his lips with her own.

There it was again, that instant response that only she could arouse from him.

He closed his arms around her, holding her close, taking comfort from the feel of her heart beating against his.

"No, we don't have to decide anything at the moment," he told her.

"Since we're not going to talk, what would you like to do in the interim?" she asked teasingly. They both knew the answer to that question.

He laughed softly, thinking how right all this felt, just as he'd thought the very same thing ten years ago. He'd been right then, as he was right now.

But maybe this time there would be a different outcome.

At least he could hope.

"Guess," he suggested.

"What do I get if I guess right?" she asked, her eyes dancing with barely suppressed mischief.

"Me," he told her.

Her grin was wide as she slid her body up against his again. "Works for me," she whispered.

Chapter Fifteen

And I'm back, Brianna thought with a suppressed sigh as she moved around the kitchen the following morning, doing her best to focus. *Back to the present. Back to reality.*

Last night, she'd gone all the way back to her last days as a high school senior, but now, perforce, she was back. Back to being the diligent nurse, the responsible single parent. Back to being the woman who did her best to be all things to everyone and slept a minimum of hours.

Last night had been about the path not taken, the one she found herself yearning for on those rare occasions when she had more than two minutes to rub together.

Staring into the refrigerator, trying to remember what it was she was looking for, Brianna wished she hadn't gone there, that she had remained firmly entrenched in the present.

As wonderful as last night was, as much as she enjoyed reliving the past, she knew the here and now would be that much more difficult to bear. Because, as full as her life was with her daughter, her father, her work, she had to admit that deep down she was lonely. Not all the time, of course—there were times when she was too exhausted to feel anything at all—but she felt that way just often enough to leave her wanting.

Grow up, for heaven's sake, she ordered herself as she took out a carton of eggs and put it on the counter.

She wasn't the wide-eyed innocent anymore, wasn't on the brink of following her dreams. She *knew* all dreams didn't come true.

All?

Heck, *most* dreams didn't come true. That was because most dreams were just that—dreams, she thought, depositing a large frying pan on the front burner. And while retaining those dreams *did* keep a person going, did give a person purpose, she freely admitted, she had embraced reality enough to know that very few ever came true.

The rest didn't have a prayer of coming true.

Ever.

And by the same token, she knew that there was no future for her with Sebastian. He had his life and she had hers. Moreover, those lives weren't separated by a few blocks or a few counties, or even states, but by half a world.

Idealistic as she once had been, Brianna was *not* so starry-eyed—or so delusional, for that matter—to think that Sebastian would give up everything he had just for her.

The adult thing was to behave as if she accepted that. To behave as if she didn't expect *anything* to change just because, for the space of one night, the earth had moved for her.

Again.

Right. Good luck with that.

It bothered him.

Brianna was acting as if nothing was different, as if last night they *hadn't* both glimpsed what could have been their lives had she not remained in Bedford when he had left.

Last night had wiped out ten years of physical estrangement and let him pick up the dropped thread. Last night had allowed him to see how very *good* it all could be.

Last night had been about beginning again. Except that now it felt as if they hadn't begun anything, just briefly revisited a world that they no longer had access to.

Still, he'd thought *because of last night* that things would be different from here on in.

Granted, he hadn't expected Brianna to slant covert looks his way and act like some love-struck puppy, but he'd expected *some* indication that last night had meant as much to her as it had to him.

Instead, what he got was the impression that it was "business as usual" for Brianna.

To begin with, when he woke up she was gone from his bed. He hadn't thought that she'd sleep in—that didn't mesh with the person she was—but he had hoped that when he opened his eyes she would be the first thing he'd see.

Instead, he saw a vacant spot beside him in his bed.

Then he realized that the pillow and comforter were neatly back in place. So neat that it gave no indication that *anyone* had been there. Had alcohol been involved last night, he might have even thought he'd imagined the whole thing, from the very first kiss to the last wildly erotic surge.

Except that he hadn't imagined it. It had been very, very real. And it had, for that stretch of time—and beyond, as she'd slept beside him and he'd lain there with his arm around her, just listening to her breathe—made him begin to entertain the idea that perhaps there were such things as do-overs.

That once in a while, people did get a second chance to get things right.

But if it all had meant so little to her that she could silently slip out of his bed without a moment's lingering, then maybe he needed to rethink his rethinking.

Two minutes after waking up, he was already in the stall, taking a quick shower rather than the lengthy one with her that he'd fallen asleep anticipating. Within five minutes he was dressed and padding down the stairs in bare feet.

He found Brianna in the kitchen, moving around between the stove and the refrigerator as if she was the one who belonged there and he was the interloper.

As if suddenly sensing his presence, she flashed him a smile. The very same smile she'd been flashing him every morning for the past week and a half. There wasn't even the slightest hint that she was holding back something extra, something special that involved only the two of them. There was no indication whatsoever that they had crossed some magic line, or gone on to a higher plateau.

"Hi," Brianna called out brightly to him. Then, nodding at the frying pan, she asked him, "What's your pleasure?"

It was on the tip of Sebastian's tongue to say, "You" in response, but he managed to keep it back, and Carrie being there, seated at the table, was only part of the reason why he'd refrained.

Carrie was an obstacle easily circumvented if he'd wanted to. The reply could have been tendered in a whisper, with him standing close enough to say the word into her ear. But something told him that the answer would have made her feel uncomfortable, so he told her, "Just coffee, thanks," and then went to the cupboard to get a mug for himself.

Every second of silence felt endless to her.

Brianna searched for something to fill the emptiness. She didn't want Sebastian thinking that she was waiting for him to make some sort of comment or reference to the night they'd shared. She didn't want him to feel on the spot and, more than that, she didn't want to become, by saying the wrong word, the object of his pity.

So, after a moment's internal debate, she went with a topic she deemed to be safe, one that would show him that she had absolutely no expectations because of last night, no demands on him whatsoever.

"So, how much longer is your vacation?" she asked cheerfully as she broke two eggs, depositing them in a bowl and then sending them scrambling about said bowl with a whisk.

"That depends on how my mother is doing," Sebastian told her. "If it looks like she's getting stronger and I feel she's getting better, then I guess I can fly back anytime."

He left his answer open-ended, really curious now to see her reaction. The girl he'd once known would want him to remain and would say as much—passionately. If she didn't, that meant he was in the presence of someone with Brianna's face, someone he didn't know at all.

Brianna chose her words carefully, wanting to convey just the right message, one he could hold on to.

"Well, I'm happy to tell you that your mother's doing remarkably well. As a matter of fact, if I didn't know any better, I would have said that there was a mistake in the initial diagnosis."

But she knew who the woman's cardiologist was and the man had an *excellent* reputation. And even though she hadn't asked to view the E.R. report—that was a matter of privacy between doctor and patient—she was well aware that the cardiologist was at the top of his game.

"Your mother doesn't behave like someone living through the aftermath of a stroke. All in all, I'd say that she's an incredibly strong woman."

She smiled, feeling this was the best possible news she could give him. "She is one of the very lucky ones," she added.

"Right," he murmured, interpreting her words in his own way.

He was right. Brianna *was* trying to get rid of him, to get him to go back to Japan. Otherwise, there would have been something else, something more. Some small attempt with perhaps a white lie to get him to remain a bit longer rather than sending him on his way.

He didn't exactly expect her to pitch herself at him bodily, but he knew her. She would have found something to make the prognosis a little more guarded than it was. After all, he'd indicated that if there was still some sort of uncertainty about his mother's condition, he could stay awhile longer. This cheerful report she'd just rendered was all but ushering him out the door. Quickly. Brianna obviously regretted what had happened between them last night.

Hey, what do you expect? a voice in his head taunted him. After all, he wasn't exactly the same inexperienced kid, either. He'd gone on, made a life for himself—of sorts—and obviously, so had she.

Last night could have very well been just a pleasant interlude for her and nothing further. Certainly not enough to make her rethink things and change her life around.

He had to assume that Brianna was happy with her life, with her daughter and with her career, and that having him around threw a crimp into all that.

Maybe she was even afraid that he would want to change things on her, place demands on her that she wasn't prepared to put up with.

No, it was better just to keep going and not look back. He certainly couldn't allow himself to daydream about building a brand-new life for himself and for her on a foundation that was all but eroding right out from beneath his feet even as he tried to take his very first steps.

Eyeing Brianna covertly to see her reaction, he said, "Well, if she's doing that well, then I guess I'm free to fly back to Tokyo."

"I guess so," she said.

Her smile was rigidly in place and she congratulated herself on not losing a beat despite the very real, very painful ache that she felt was eating up her gut from the inside out.

Brianna was well aware that it wasn't exactly ethical to use his mother as an excuse to stay. She couldn't lie to him about her condition. But wasn't all fair in love and war?

This wasn't war, she reminded herself and then quietly acknowledged that it really wasn't exactly love, either.

At least, not for him. He'd leave the first chance he got.

For her it was a whole different story but it was *not*

a story that she was about to share with Sebastian—or with anyone.

It was *her* story to bear, *her* problem to deal with and resolve. And maybe, if she didn't involve anyone else in it, she might bring about a good conclusion.

Or so she hoped.

"Well, if you're going to be shoving off soon, maybe you'd better spend a little more time with your mother," she suggested brightly, still doing her best to maintain a cheerful countenance. "Otherwise, she's going to feel neglected—and we want her as upbeat as possible, even though, quite honestly, just the thought of you leaving will probably take its toll on her." *As well as on me,* she added silently.

"Right," Sebastian agreed mechanically.

About to leave the room, he turned around to the counter and retrieved the steaming mug of coffee he'd just poured for himself. Without thinking, he paused to take a sip of the hot, inky liquid. As it wound a warm, bracing path through his esophagus, down to his stomach, he looked in Brianna's direction.

"Good coffee," he murmured.

"Thanks. I thought you might like it." She addressed the words to his departing back.

His coffee preference was, even after all this time, one of the things she remembered about him—one of the *many* things she remembered about him, she silently amended. Sebastian took his coffee strong, hot and as black as potting soil—the exact opposite of the way she took hers. She liked her coffee exceedingly pale, with sugar and enough cream to make the cup pass for chocolate milk—light chocolate milk.

Out of the corner of her eye, as she watched Sebastian leave the room—doing her best to prepare for the moment when he would be leaving her life again—she became aware that Carrie had wiggled down off her seat and was now pushing the step stool up against the counter.

The next second, the little girl scrambled up the three steps that allowed her to touch a few things on the counter.

In this case, it was a loaf of bread that had her attention.

"What are you up to?" Brianna asked her daughter, forcing herself to focus on something other than Sebastian and his inevitable departure.

"I'm gonna make some toast," Carrie declared matter-of-factly.

While she was all for encouraging independence in children no matter how young, this was different. She was in no mood to deal with the myriad of difficulties that could come out of the seemingly simple undertaking of making toast.

"That's okay—I've got it," Brianna said.

"No, you don't," Carrie contradicted her, surprising her.

Brianna looked at the little girl quizzically. "Why would you say that?"

"Because you're busy staring at Sebastian." It wasn't an accusation, but a statement of fact.

"No, I'm not," she protested with just enough feeling to sound sincere rather than confused, which she still was regarding Carrie's behavior.

"Yes, you are," Carrie insisted. "You're watching him walk out. Why? Are you afraid he's going to fall down and hurt himself?" She asked the only thing that seemed to make logical sense to her.

"No," Brianna told her patiently.

But I'm afraid that I am. Or have already. I'm afraid that I've fallen in love with him all over again—harder this time—and I shouldn't have.

"Then why are you watching him leave the room, Mama?" Carrie asked.

"I wasn't watching him leave the room," Brianna lied. "I was just thinking."

"About what?" Carrie asked.

"About what to give a little girl who asks so many questions for breakfast," she told her, pointedly looking at her daughter.

"Scrambled eggs, toast and bacon," her daughter recited.

Because she asked for the same thing *every* morning, Brianna's voice blended in with Carrie's, reinforcing the choice.

Carrie broke down in giggles.

And that, Brianna hoped, was the end of the little girl's interrogations.

At least for now.

Chapter Sixteen

Sebastian was upstairs packing.

Which meant that he would be leaving soon, Brianna thought with a heavy heart. Maybe even by tomorrow. She hadn't been able to get herself to ask exactly when. All she knew was that it meant that she'd been right about the other night. It had just happened. It meant nothing to him.

She meant nothing to him.

Despite the fact that she'd told herself that all along, her heart hurt.

When the doorbell rang, she was tempted just to ignore it, but whoever was on the other side of the door might be coming to see Mrs. Hunter. If she let them continue ringing the doorbell, it might make her come down the stairs to answer it herself. Although she was pretty certain that Mrs. Hunter was feeling far better than she pretended, she still didn't want the woman exerting herself.

Still she hurried to answer before the doorbell rang a third time. She did *not* expect to see her father standing on the doorstep. "Dad, what are you doing here?"

Jim MacKenzie looked around as he walked in. "I thought I'd take Carrie home with me for the night," he told her. Still not seeing the little girl, he looked at Brianna and asked, "Where is she?"

Brianna nodded toward the stairs. "Keeping my patient company." A fond smile curved her lips as she thought of the duo. "She and Mrs. Hunter really seem to have hit it off."

"Yes, I know." Her father laughed softly to himself. "She's a pistol, our little girl."

Brianna looked at him, confused. "You know?" she questioned. To the best of her knowledge, she hadn't said anything to her father regarding the situation. "How do you know?"

That was a slip, he thought. Brianna didn't know he'd been in touch with Barbara Hunter, didn't know anything about the nature of what had brought the two of them together in the first place, and he had a feeling that now was not the time to tell her.

"Doesn't matter," he said dismissively. "I thought I'd give you the night off by taking Carrie home with me for the night. I rented some of her favorite animated movies. Thought she might get a kick out of some one-on-one time with her old grandpa."

"How's that giving me the night off?" she asked. "Officially, I'm taking care of Mrs. Hunter. Carrie's good about entertaining herself. She usually hangs out in a corner, reading her books until it's time for her to go to bed."

"Barbara's got to sleep some time," he pointed out. "And then you get the night off—to spend it the way you want," he added, looking at her significantly.

Her suspicions were definitely aroused. Her father did *not* number among the most subtle people on the planet. "And just exactly how would I want to spend it, Dad?" she asked.

His wide shoulders moved up and down in a nonchalant shrug that seemed just a tad too innocent. "Oh, I don't know, maybe with Sebastian. As I recall, you two *were* going together before my accident."

"The operative word here being *were,*" she pointed out. Her eyes narrowed as she looked at her father more intently. "What are you up to, Dad?"

He supposed if he didn't tell her, they were going to dance around the subject all evening, wasting too much time. "All right, Bree, if you want me to be blunt about it—"

"Please, be blunt," she instructed, waiting to hear just what he was plotting.

"I'm trying to give the two of you some alone time— together," he threw in just in case Brianna was going to twist his words around.

A sad smile curved the corners of her mouth.

"That's very sweet of you, Dad, but you could have

saved yourself the trouble of coming here. Sebastian's in his room packing. His mother is doing very well, so he's ready to go back to his life and I really doubt that there's much of a reason for me to be here much longer anyway."

She saw that the last piece of information didn't seem to surprise her father. There was only one reason for that.

"She never really had heart trouble, did she?" She didn't wait for him to answer her. "Dad, if this is some kind of a plot that the two of you cooked up, I'm afraid you've been wasting your time. Sebastian's going back to Japan."

He'd never known his daughter to give up on anything easily. "In the words of the immortal and far-wiser-than-given-credit-for Yogi Berra, 'It ain't over till it's over.'"

Brianna sighed. She was *not* about to knock her head against a stone wall. "Well, it's over. Trust me," she said with finality.

Her father stared at her in complete disbelief. "So that's it?" he asked incredulously. "You're just giving up? You, the girl who kept kicking me in the behind because I said the doctors were right? The girl who said she absolutely refused to let me give up?"

She'd already accepted defeat—why couldn't he? "That was different," she insisted.

"How?" Jim asked. "How was that different from this?"

Why was he making this so hard for her? "Because it

just was. For one thing, you didn't have a life waiting for you in Japan. You were intent on resigning from life."

"But you told me I had a choice. A choice," he repeated. "And Sebastian has a choice. Just like I did," he maintained.

Maybe so, she thought, but he'd picked the wrong one. "Well, he's choosing to leave," she told her father, struggling to keep her voice from quavering.

No matter what she said, Jim found that really difficult to believe. "Did you tell him how you feel?" he prodded.

More than anything, Brianna wanted to deny that she felt anything at all, but that would be lying and she had never lied to her father.

"If he doesn't know by now..." She let her voice trail off, but her meaning was clear.

"So you didn't tell him," her father concluded. He sighed, shaking his head. "Honey, because I love you, I'm going to tell you something that's going to violate the sacred man-code." He leaned into her and said in a stage whisper, "We don't read minds—and when it comes to relationships, we need all the help, all the outright hints we can get." He looked at her pointedly. "For God's sake, *tell* him how you feel. Ask him to stay— unless you don't want him to," he qualified, never taking his eyes off his daughter.

It was a choice between saving face and telling the truth. Since this was her father, she was forced to go with the truth.

"Of course I want him to stay, but wanting him to isn't enough."

He'd always bragged to everyone that his daughter was incredibly bright—but not this time. "I think you're wrong there."

"Dad, what if I ask him to stay…and he tells me he can't? Or he won't?" Which would have been even worse to bear.

"You'll never know unless you put yourself out there, Bree." His eyes, so like hers, held her captive. "And he won't tell you he can't stay." He looked at her and said with conviction, "I know that for a fact."

"How? How do you know that?" she demanded, feeling her heart fluttering in her chest, drawing hope. "Did he say something to you?" Not that she thought that was even remotely possible. When would he be talking to her father? And why?

"No," he told her, "he didn't say anything to me."

She was aware of how carefully he phrased his reply. "Then to who?" she asked, the edge of her temper becoming frayed.

Jim debated not saying anything further. But if he didn't, his daughter would allow the love of her life to leave—for a second time.

Jim made his decision. "Sebastian intimated as much to his mother."

"His mother?" she echoed, stunned. "When did you talk to his mother?" And then she amended her question. "*Why* are you talking to his mother? Dad, what's going on here?"

"Nothing," Jim lamented, "if the two of you continue to insist on remaining in second gear."

"Dad, ten years have gone by since Sebastian and I were 'together,' as you put it," she protested. "We missed our chance."

"Who says you only get one chance?" he pressed, then insisted, "Honey, you *have* been given a second chance. It's up to the two of you to take advantage of it. Look at it this way," he advised. "Maybe everything that happened happened for a reason. If it hadn't, you would have missed out on having Carrie in your life and Carrie would have wound up being swallowed up by the system. You also wouldn't have become the wonderful nurse that you are today.

"And maybe," he speculated, "things were supposed to go this long, roundabout route so that Barbara and I would get together."

A medium-size feather could have easily knocked her over. "You and Barbara," she repeated, utterly stunned by his revelation. "Together?"

"Yes. Me and Barbara. We've been keeping company," he told her quaintly. "And to tell the truth, I've been thinking of asking her to marry me."

Maybe a small feather rather than a medium-size one. "When did all this happen?" she cried. Had she been completely blind and oblivious to everything? Or had they been seeing one another covertly? She was usually far more observant than this.

"I don't run everything past you," Jim told his daughter. "It's enough for you to know it happened—and that

I'm hoping you won't disappoint me and become a by-stander in your own life." He looked at her significantly. "Now, go and get your second chance while I go and spend some quality time with my granddaughter—" he smiled broadly "—and my girl."

Because he definitely appeared to be looking past her shoulder, Brianna turned around. What she saw was Carrie walking into the room. She was holding on to Barbara's hand. A very hale-and-hearty-looking Barbara, she noted.

There was a glow about the older woman when she looked at her father. They definitely had a connection, Brianna thought.

"Grandpa is going to make dinner for Mrs. Hunter and me," Carrie announced cheerfully. "And then we're going to watch *Little People,*" she added, referring to a popular children's movie that had just hit the DVD market.

Carrie seemed so excited, Brianna didn't have the heart to say anything except, "Well, have a good time, honey." Bending down to her level, she gave the little girl a warm hug and kissed her. Carrie dutifully stood still for it, even though it looked as if she wanted to wiggle free.

"You, too, dear," Barbara told her significantly as Brianna rose back to her feet.

Her father offered Sebastian's mother his arm, which the older woman readily accepted, slipping her own through his.

"Don't wait up," her father told her with a wink.

And then just like that, he, Carrie and Sebastian's mother were gone.

Brianna stood there for a moment in the silent house, staring at the closed door and mulling over her father's words. She debated whether to ignore them—or act on them.

She chewed on her lower lip nervously. What if her father was wrong?

What if he was right and she did nothing?

Torn, Brianna decided that if she didn't confront Sebastian about her feelings, if she let this moment just slide by and slip into oblivion, she would never forgive herself.

Bracing her shoulders, she took a deep breath and went up the stairs. She felt as if she was walking up to his door in slow motion. Even so, she couldn't get herself to knock right away.

Instead, she stood there for a moment—maybe even several minutes—arguing with herself in silence.

This was getting her nowhere. Since when was she such a coward? Brianna silently demanded.

Biting off a choice word, she knocked on the door.

The moment she did, the door flew open and she found herself looking up into Sebastian's soul-melting brown eyes.

How was she going to face not seeing him again?

The sudden sharp ache in her abdomen answered the question for her. She wasn't going to face it. She couldn't. Not without a fight.

"Something wrong, Bree?" he asked her. "Is it my

mother?" he asked, suddenly thinking the worst. That was where his thoughts were going as he packed, to the worst scenarios. He realized that what he was really trying to do was talk himself into staying a little longer.

And not just because of his mother...

"No, she's fine. Really," she assured him. *Okay, then what are you going to tell him about why you're standing in his doorway?* She searched for an answer. "I just thought I'd pop in for a second...to see if you needed any help packing," she concluded, looking at the open suitcase on the bed.

Turning, Sebastian followed her line of vision and then shrugged. He'd been at it for a while, moving in slow motion.

"I was never very good at packing," he confessed.

"Maybe that's because you don't want to go," she suggested matter-of-factly. Brianna held her breath, waiting for his reaction—knowing she was going out on a long, shaky limb.

Sebastian eyed her sharply. Was he that transparent? "What makes you say that?"

Brianna sighed, wavering. She debated backtracking. But she'd come this far, so she might as well go the distance.

"Wishful thinking," she answered quietly.

Sebastian realized he was holding his breath. "By wishful thinking you mean—"

"That I don't want you to go, okay?" she finally blurted out.

Her answer made him laugh. "That's funny, because

I really don't want to go," he heard himself confessing. Once the words were out, he felt a huge sense of relief.

She didn't understand. This whole day, he'd seemed so focused on leaving. "But then why are you packing?" she asked.

"Because if I stay, I might get used to it, used to being here with you—"

She was still waiting to hear something convincing. "And that would be bad because…?"

Pacing now, Sebastian blew out a breath. "Because I have no right to think that you could forgive me for allowing us to drift apart the way I did."

The fault wasn't his alone, she thought now. "It takes two to drift," Brianna pointed out. "And if you forgive me, I'll forgive you," she told him, still holding her breath, still waiting to see if she'd made a mistake by being so honest with him.

"That easy?" he asked, amused despite himself.

Brianna watched him for a long moment. She wasn't sure if he was being serious or not, but she knew that she was, at least about the forgiving part. She wanted no more stumbling blocks, no more obstacles in their way. They'd already lost too much time. To lose more would only be compounding the sin, adding insult to injury.

"That easy," she assured him with a smile.

Overwhelmed, relieved, Sebastian impulsively took her into his arms and kissed her.

And then stopped abruptly.

He couldn't afford to let himself get carried away, no matter how much he wanted to. It was too early in the evening. He was certain that both Carrie and his mother were still awake.

"Something on your mind?" she asked, mentally crossing her fingers that, whatever it was, it wasn't going to make him back away from her.

His grin seemed positively wicked and instantly got to her, speeding up her pulse even more than his kiss just had.

"Lots," Sebastian confessed. "But it's going to have to wait for a few hours."

She had a feeling she knew exactly what he was thinking, so she told him with confidence, "No, it doesn't."

"Oh?" And then he noticed that, although his bedroom door was now open, he didn't hear any noise coming from outside his room.

Curious, he stepped out into the hallway. The sound of the TV, the hum of voices, a radio on somewhere— none of those typical noises were audible to him tonight.

He looked at Brianna and asked, "Where is everyone?"

"Out," she answered simply, unable to suppress the smile that insisted on playing on her lips.

"Carrie and my mother are both out?" he questioned. His mother was recovering from a stroke. Why had Brianna let her go out by herself? Or worse, with Carrie?

"Carrie and your mother are both out," she repeated. Then, to set his mind at ease, she explained, "My father came by and took Carrie and your mother back to his house for dinner and an animated movie."

He could see her father taking Carrie home for that, but his mother as well? It didn't make any sense.

"He took my mother?" he asked incredulously. "You're sure?"

"I'm sure," she answered glibly, then let him in on the rest of it. "It seems that the two of them have been 'keeping company,' to use my father's words."

For a second, Sebastian's mouth dropped open. He hadn't thought that the two even knew one another. "Since when?"

"Since a while, apparently," she told him. "Actually, I think my dad's getting ready to ask you for your blessings."

His brow furrowed as he tried to make sense out of what she'd just told him. "Exactly what is it that I'm blessing?"

"What do you think?" she teased. Then, to make sure that there was no misunderstanding, she added, "I think those two crazy kids want to get married."

"Now you're kidding me."

The next moment, he was surprised to see Brianna shaking her head. "Nope. I'm being serious. They're being serious," she specified. "It looks like you're the only one here who isn't serious."

As if taking his cue, Sebastian pulled her back into his arms, this time with the reassuring knowledge that they were alone and would remain that way for at least several hours to come.

"Who says?" he challenged.

She could feel her body heating up already. "Well then, why don't you put your money where your mouth is?"

The expression on Sebastian's face sent her pulse scrambling in heated anticipation. "I'd rather put my mouth where yours is."

"That, too," she encouraged seductively.

He began to lower his mouth, then stopped one more time. "Oh, by the way—"

"Yes?" she asked, trying hard not to sound as impatient as she felt.

"Will you finally marry me?"

"Any time, any place," she told him without the slightest hesitation. "Now, shut up and make love with me before I jump you."

"Promises, promises." He laughed, then said far more seriously, "Gladly."

It was the last word either one of them said for a very long, satisfying time.

* * * * *

*Don't miss Marie Ferrarella's next romance,
CAVANAUGH ON DUTY, available May 2013
from Harlequin Romantic Suspense.*

#2257 A WEAVER VOW
Return to the Double C
Allison Leigh
When Erik Clay makes a commitment, it is forever, and when he meets Isabella Lockhart, he knows forever is what he wants. Unfortunately, there's an eleven-year-old boy whose heart is just as bruised as Isabella's standing squarely in their way....

#2258 EXPECTING FORTUNE'S HEIR
The Fortunes of Texas: Southern Invasion
Cindy Kirk
Shane Fortune is accustomed to women using his family for money, so when the cute and spunky Lia Serrano tells him that she is pregnant with his baby after a one-night stand, he is seriously skeptical. But after spending more time together, he can't help but hope the baby is truly his....

#2259 MADE IN TEXAS!
Byrds of a Feather
Crystal Green
After inheriting a share of property, independent woman Donna Byrd came to Texas to build a B&B. She'd help market the inn then head right back to her city life...at least, that was the plan until she met cowboy Caleb Granger!

#2260 A DADDY FOR DILLON
Men of the West
Stella Bagwell
Ranch foreman Laramie Jones's life is all work and no play, until Leyla Chee arrives as the ranch's new chef with her young son in tow. It's true that Laramie has won little Dillon's admiration, but can he charm the protective mommy, too?

#2261 THE TEXAN'S SURPRISE BABY
Gina Wilkins
After a passionate one-night stand with dashing Texas P.I. Andrew Walker, the commitment-shy Hannah Bell refuses to see the relationship go any further. Six months later, their paths cross again, but this time he has a surprisingly special reason to win Hannah's heart....

#2262 FATHER BY CHOICE
Amanda Berry
On the verge of a promotion, workaholic Brady Ward learns that he has a seven-year-old daughter living with her mother—his ex, Maggie!—in a small town. Can the big-city businessman ditch the climb up the corporate ladder for a simpler life with the family he never knew he had?

HSECNM0413

REQUEST YOUR FREE BOOKS!
2 FREE NOVELS PLUS 2 FREE GIFTS!

⊞ HARLEQUIN®

SPECIAL EDITION
Life, Love & Family

HSE13

***

Murphy, please don't get into more trouble.

Whatever had made her think she could be a better parent to Murphy than his other options? He needed a man around, not just a woman he could barely tolerate.

He needed his father.

And now all they had was each other.

Isabella Lockhart couldn't bear to think about it.

"It was an accident!" Murphy yelled. "Dude! That's my bat. You can't just take my bat!"

"I just did, *dude*," the man returned flatly. He closed his hand over Murphy's thin shoulder and forcibly moved him away from Isabella.

Isabella rounded on the man, gaping at him. He was wearing a faded brown ball cap and aviator sunglasses that hid his eyes. "Take your hand off him! Who do you think you are?"

"The man your boy decided to aim at with his blasted baseball." His jaw was sharp and shadowed by brown stubble and his lips were thinned.

"I did not!" Murphy screamed right into Isabella's ear.

She winced, then pointed. "Go sit down."

She drew in a calming breath and turned her head into the breeze that she'd begun to suspect never died here in Weaver, Wyoming, before facing the man again. "I'm Isabella Lockhart," she began.

"I know who you are."

She'd been in Weaver only a few weeks, but it really was a small town if people she'd never met already knew who she was.

"I'm sure we can resolve whatever's happened here, Mr. uh—?"

"Erik Clay."

Focusing on the woman in front of him was a lot safer than focusing on the skinny black-haired hellion sprawled on Ruby's bench.

She tucked her white-blond hair behind her ear with a visibly shaking hand. Bleached blond, he figured, considering the eyes that she turned toward the back of his truck were such a dark brown they were nearly black.

Even angry as he was, he wasn't blind to the whole effect. Weaver's newcomer was a serious looker.

***

Don't miss A WEAVER VOW
by USA TODAY bestselling author Allison Leigh.

Available in May 2013 from
Harlequin® Special Edition® wherever books are sold.

SPECIAL EDITION

Life, Love and Family

EXPECTING FORTUNE'S HEIR
by Cindy Kirk

Shane Fortune is accustomed to women using his
family for money, so when the cute and spunky
Lia Serrano tells him that she is pregnant with his
baby after a one-night stand, he is seriously skeptical.
But after spending more time together, he can't help
but hope the baby is truly his....

Look for the next book in
The Fortunes of Texas:
Southern Invasion

Available in May from Harlequin Special Edition,
wherever books are sold.

HSE65740

SPECIAL EDITION

Life, Love and Family

MADE IN TEXAS!
by Crystal Green

After inheriting a share of property, independent
woman Donna Byrd came to Texas to build a
B and B. She'd help market the inn then head right
back to her city life…at least, that was the plan until
she met cowboy Caleb Granger!

Look for the next story in the
Byrds of a Feather
miniseries next month.

Available in May 2013 from Harlequin Special Edition,
wherever books are sold.

www.Harlequin.com

HSE65741